RECEIVED
APR 2 1 2009

Revenant

Tristan Hughes was born in Atikokan, Canada and brought up around Llangoed, Ynys Mon where he currently lives. *Revenant* is his third novel.

D1403123

property of
The Blue Mountains
Public Library
L.E. Shore Memorial Library
Thornbury, Ontario N0H 2P0

Also by Tristan Hughes

The Tower
Send My Cold Bones Home

RECEIVED

Revenant

Tristan Hughes

PICADOR

First published 2008 by Picador

First published in paperback 2008 by Picador
an imprint of Pan Macmillan Ltd
Pan Macmillan, 20 New Wharf Road, London N1 9RR
Basingstoke and Oxford
Associated companies throughout the world
www.panmacmillan.com

ISBN 978-0-330-45196-3

Copyright © Tristan Hughes 2008

The right of Tristan Hughes to be identified as the
author of this work has been asserted by him in accordance
with the Copyright, Designs and Patents Act 1988.

All rights reserved. No part of this publication may be
reproduced, stored in or introduced into a retrieval system, or
transmitted, in any form, or by any means (electronic, mechanical,
photocopying, recording or otherwise) without the prior written
permission of the publisher. Any person who does any unauthorized
act in relation to this publication may be liable to criminal
prosecution and civil claims for damages.

9 8 7 6 5 4 3 2 1

A CIP catalogue record for this book is available from
the British Library.

Typeset by Intype Libra Ltd
Printed and bound in Great Britain by
Mackays of Chatham plc, Chatham, Kent

This book is sold subject to the condition that it shall not,
by way of trade or otherwise, be lent, re-sold, hired out,
or otherwise circulated without the publisher's prior consent
in any form of binding or cover other than that in which
it is published and without a similar condition including this
condition being imposed on the subsequent purchaser.

Visit **www.picador.com** to read more about all our books
and to buy them. You will also find features, author interviews and
news of any author events, and you can sign up for e-newsletters
so that you're always first to hear about our new releases.

PART ONE

Arrivals

Neil

In the springtime the old people come back. They arrive as soon as the grass starts to grow and the daffodils sprout by the roadsides. As the sun becomes warm once more they suddenly appear, shuffling stiffly around the edges of the town as though they had never left, as though they were cold-blooded things that had spent the winter hidden away in nooks and crannies and clammy, secret caves. The light seems to dazzle them to begin with. They keep their heads bent down and their eyes fixed firmly on the ground, watching their first weak and tentative steps, a little afraid perhaps that their legs will fail them, or that they will not quite remember how to use them. But on they go, inching unseeing past the tea-houses and the shops and the grey walls of the castle until at last they become more confident in their weak strides and arch their wrinkled faces towards the sun, feeding on its beams like iguanas, and make their blinking way towards the sea, always the sea.

Look at them – these ancient water-gazers, these withered lilies that bloom on the fronts of seaside towns. They must have returned as I slept. Because when I woke this morning a premonitory scent had already crept its way into my room: a faint mix of lavender and stale urine, the gentle musk of mouldy furniture, a pot-pourri of dying cells. It's their smell. There's a delicate, carrion reek to it that makes the seagulls bold this time of year and they were screeching greedily above the rooftops. I tried to smother the noise with my blankets but it was useless and before I knew it I was wide awake and the air around me was horridly alive with their shrieking travesty of a morning chorus. How I hate these birds, hate them, with their malevolent, yellow eyes and the splatter of blood on the bottom of their beaks! Sometimes I think they've caterwauled their way through my whole life, have hovered about it like the aquatic vultures that they are, watching each step I've ever taken, waiting for them to weaken and falter so they can swoop. Imagine ending your days on their oily, fishy tongues! I can imagine nothing worse. When the moment arrives I will be sure to give myself to the crematorium's fire and afterwards be scattered from my urn; at the most I will become ashes in their mouths.

The spring should bring back swallows and lambs and the viridian glimmer of leaf-buds, but when I opened my curtains I could see none of these. I could only see them: straggled out in ones and twos along the promenade, swaying slightly in a breeze that was hardly strong enough to lurch through my open window. It was too feeble even to ruffle the straits into which they stared. Its waters remained sluggish and flat and greasily still, a rancid sea-soup with damp strands of bladderwrack lolling around its edges like clusters of dead eggs. While across the straits, on the mainland shore, the mountains bulged out like the bloated bellies of drowned giants – who would never wake up.

After a few minutes of looking it was as if my eyeballs had fallen into some gloopy, stagnant pool. I was seeing everything in slow, syrupy motion, and I began to wonder if perhaps my vision was becoming empathetic somehow, if it were not possible that I might be seeing the world as the old people saw it. My taid said that his eyes got slower as he got older, that they caught down with the movement of his body and like a good dancer's adjusted themselves to the stiff, arthritic rhythm of his limbs. He told me it was one of nature's ways of compensating the creatures to whom it gave such a cramped and finite span of life, because it stretched time out near the end, or at least provided an optical illusion of duration. He was a kind man, my taid – to humans anyway – and I miss the way he glossed the truth for me with a glass half full even when I knew it was half empty too, even when I had seen how his slowed senses elongated his nightmares and made time the rack he was tortured on.

Once, when I was a child, me and my friends found a bicycle embedded in the mud below the tideline. It was almost new, in perfect working order, and by chance had come to rest entirely upright in the sludge, as though its rider had just that second got their wheels stuck and gone headlong over the handlebars into the salty mire. It was quite a find for us, and in our excitement we began riding it there and then in the mud, taking turns to pedal it forward a foot or two until the wheels stuck fast again and it squelched to a halt. On and on we went, making our inchmeal way towards where the shore became stony and solid. But in the end it was just too far. We were so wet and filthy and exhausted that the last ten yards were beyond us. We couldn't even muster the strength to pick the bicycle up and carry it, and instead hid it beneath some seaweed and arranged to collect it later. The next morning it had vanished as mysteriously as it had appeared. But it is not that which I remember so much as the walk home that day, how my body trembled with tiredness, how sapped and wobbly my legs were, as though the mud still enveloped them and held back my every step. And I now realized that it was this same feeling of leaden fatigue that had settled into my eyes, spreading out through my vision and down through my limbs, making it almost impossible for me to pull back from the window and retract my gaze. As I stared, the figures of the old people seemed to harden in front of me like the bars of a cage.

And then I saw movement. Only a glimpse at first, a furtive whirl of cherry-blossom pink that tumbled suddenly from behind the ice-cream booth by the entrance to the pier and reeled along across the edge of the town green. There were several cars parked on the grass and it bobbed between them, flickering in and out of view, stopping and starting, crouching and jumping, until finally it made a frantic dash on to the open spaces of the green and resolved itself into the hyperactive blur of a young girl's legs. She was running from some invisible pursuer, or pursuers, whom I quickly identified as two dull-witted little boys who were still poking about behind the ice-cream booth. She was miles ahead of their seeking now and no longer bothered to hide. Exhilarated by her own momentum, she zigzagged towards the promenade, with her hair bouncing on her head and her tee-shirt and skirt flapping about around her skinny body. In a blink she'd arrived at the sea front and started weaving her helter-skelter way through the stooped shadows of the watchers. Her buoyancy seemed to stir them. They twisted their necks to face her. They smiled. Some held out crooked fingers in her wake, as though they were belatedly reaching for the children who had run away from them into middle age.

But there was no catching her. She jumped down off the sea wall on to the narrow strip of sand that the tide had rolled out for her, and flung herself, elatedly, into a cartwheel. For a fraction of a second the tiny white triangle of her knickers seemed to hover like a tern's wing above the water, and it was just a fraction, but it was enough to bring her back. In dread I saw her face become similar, and then the same. Everything else followed: her hair, her legs, her arms, until it could only be her – running again to the water's edge as the gulls began to gather in ravening circles in the sky and the breeze came alive and licked the surface of the sea. Running again into the swell that now slouched its way shorewards and grabbed hold of her ankles. And I tried to move but I couldn't. And I tried to call out but I couldn't. And there they were, watching while it happened, exactly as they had before. I tried so hard to do something but it was like I was buried alive, or under an ocean with a thousand weeds tightening around my limbs, and it was then I realized that I was not seeing the world as the old people did but as she had, from beneath the water, looking up at the bleared figures of those who watched but couldn't see and didn't come.

Ricky

Croeso, it said. Welcome. Welcome home, Ricky my son. And they must of taught me well 'cause I didn't need to read the English bit.

I don't know when they put the new sign up but it's in a good spot, there on the side of the pass-over. That's new too, I think. But I can't be certain – it's been a while, it's been a hell of a while. They used to have a sign on the train platform at Prestatyn. That I remember. A battered, weathered old thing, with the paint all blistered and peeling. It was sad really. There was this picture of a red dragon on it and they'd tried to make it look dead friendly: big, welcoming smile, potbelly, arms spread out to hug you, that kind of stuff – Christ! he might've even been holding a frigging balloon. But they'd only half succeeded, I'm telling you, because dead is what he looked. Or maybe not quite completely dead but well on his way, like they'd taken out his claws and fangs and cut off his balls, so he'd given up the fight and decided to end it all in Prestatyn, getting fat on hot dogs and drunk on cheap cider and giving balloons to children he would've torn to shreds in his prime. Poor bastard.

You won't believe this, but my great-grandmother used to own a dancing bear. I'm not joking or nothing – a bona fide dancing bear. Llewelyn she called it, after the prince. And they say it was just like that dragon: neutered to shit, not a sharp bit left on it.

Croeso, it said. But Queensferry, Buckley – they're hardly a welcome, are they, no sight for sore eyes. I'm always telling people I meet that I come from this beautiful place; straight off a postcard I'll say, a real hidden gem, sparkling full of valleys, mountains and beaches. And if I've had a few I'll wax positively lyrical: it'll get greener by the minute, it'll be summer all the time, and the only risk of rain'll be from the tears of nostalgia dripping off my lashes. Ricky's lost wonderland. Ricky's Wales. But fuck, if they'd followed me across the border today they'd be thinking, that Ricky, he don't half talk a load of shite. Wonderland my arse, neverland more like – never-ever land. We might as well be in Slough, they'd think, not this semi-Scouse sprawl, not this eyesore of warehouses and factories and slip-roads, not this armpit at the end of the M56. Which is harsh, maybe. There's worse spots on this big island of ours, much worse. I'll vouch for it. I've been to a fair few of them myself. It's just none of them seem to get me down like this one, to leave a sad feeling in the pit of my belly and make me press my foot on the accelerator and keep my attention slap bang on the road ahead.

I suppose it's the expectation, isn't it? You've crossed a border and it's supposed to be different, but it doesn't look it. I've come this far and I should be home, but I'm not, not yet anyway. And that's what makes these places seem kind of more depressing than others – greyer, grimier, grimmer – like you've put on a DVD thinking it's going to be in glorious Technicolor and it turns out to be in crappy black and white.

Which *is* harsh, I grant you – only let's be honest here: border towns *are* almost always depressing. You're *supposed* to cross through them. They're not there to tempt you to stop. And the ones who don't keep going, the ones who dawdle betwixt and be-frigging-tween, well, no wonder they're depressed. You would be too if everyone else was passing by, off on some jaunt or other, trying not to look you straight in the glum, black and white eye. I mean, have you ever seen a happy face in customs or passport control? No, they're all sullen, moody fuckers, aren't they? And in my experience people in border towns are moodier, broodier, and just plain sodding meaner, than other folks. Do a poll or something, and I bet you find there's more piss-heads and scrapping per capita in them than anywhere else. Take my advice: if you get the choice live somewhere people go to – or leave from, at least – and don't hang about on the edge like a rusty hinge. Or if not be a proper nomad, like them Masai fellers from Africa. Or like old Llew, who I never saw, but who keeps on shuffling in and out of my head for some reason, padding along on his clawless paws, gnashing his toothless gums, pausing to prance a jig or two.

It's funny how you remember things. Some stuff is there all the time, lurking around beneath the surface, while other stuff just flits through – here one second, gone the next. I was chatting to this doctor bloke once and he tried explaining to me how my brain was full of electricity, millions of pulses of it, and that if he put a monitor on it it'd look like a Christmas tree or one of those aerial pictures of cities at night. And these pulses, he says, well, they're my thoughts, and they leap from place to place, from cell to cell, and they leave tracks behind them – don't ask me how – and these are my memories. Which is all very well and good, but he still couldn't tell me why some of them stuck about and others didn't, why some of them made guest appearances while others were there for the whole fucking run. And I didn't like to mention it at the time – because he looked pretty pleased with himself for being so clever and sober enough to speak – but what's the use knowing how something works if you haven't really got a clue what it does or why it does it? Congratulations, Ricky, you've got a generator inside your skull! Thanks, Doc. So what does it do? It generates. And? It generates. For?

Because? Look, Ricky, maybe yours isn't fired up right tonight, but try running this through it nice and slowly: it generates *because it's a generator*! Cheers, Doc. And I didn't like to mention it either – because everyone else looked pretty happy with themselves for understanding his pearls of smarmy wisdom and I didn't want to dampen their spirits – but if I've got this amazing piece of machinery on top of my neck then why the fuck does it spend ninety per cent of its time churning out and storing crap? And not just trivial crap either, but bad crap.

And would you credit it but here I am today, driving back, with Queensferry dragging me into a downer and old Llew doing a clumsy two-step across my cerebellum, when my trusty generator clicks into gear and comes up with its own theory: that my brain is full of roads and border towns, and most of the good stuff in it – the memories that make you chuckle for a second to yourself, or at least don't make you feel any worse than you already do – doesn't stay put, it keeps on the roads (maybe it is the roads) and fizzes along them like champagne bubbles; and the stuff that lingers, the sulky sediment that's stopped and settled behind its border town windows, well that's the bad stuff.

Then I look up and find I'm on top of the pass, with the Clwyd valley sweeping below me. It's appeared so suddenly that it's like one of those magical places that kids stumble into in books. There's this patchwork of fields and rolling hills with a hint of mist hazing them, and these trees – proper ones: oaks, beeches, none of your suburban twigs – that seem to float out of them and be solid at the same time, like they've sprouted half from the ground and half from the air, like you might expect to see a troupe of fairies frolicking around them and a unicorn munching on acorns. And I'm wondering why it's surprised me but I know it hasn't, not really. And I realize I've forgotten it was here (a good sign, according to my theory anyway), but I haven't actually forgotten at all because I knew it was. And then it comes to me – that somehow, the whole time I've been driving, all the way from Acton, I've been waiting for my Wales to happen, to turn up, but because I was waiting it didn't. You see, it's a shy, furtive kind of beast to begin with, this place I'm from, and it doesn't appreciate the glare of lights and the blare of trumpets; it doesn't like to be announced, not by a sign or a map or anything like that. No, it's like one of them rare animals in nature programmes, the ones they spend ages trying to film but who don't show up; and then, the moment they switch their cameras off and pack up their gear, it does – it shimmies right into view and gives them all a wave.

For a few minutes my heart's just bursting. I'm going down into the valley thinking why has it taken me this long, why have I put it off, why have I held it at arm's length and let it hide from me behind England's undergrowth, why has it taken Steph to hunt me out and call me back? That letter. That letter that never in a year of bloody Sundays did I expect. Hiya, Ricky, it's Steph . . . Hiya, Ricky, it's a miracle.

But for now it's just bursting. And for these few minutes this is my wonderland. Llew ambles past, smiling, shaking a tambourine. That dragon from Prestatyn, he's leapt right out of his picture to join me, and he's young again – fit, reborn, roaring fire. Because even though there's a slight mist on the horizon, I can see it all. There's the mountains to my left, the sea to my right, coming together inch by inch, mile by mile, until they almost meet at Penmaenmawr. There's the Great Orme, worming its way into the water. There's Seiriol's Island, with its lonely tower. And there's my island, and it's just as green and beautiful as I told those bastards it was. Fuck, I don't even need a car for this journey; I can make it the rest of the way in my head. Across the bridge and over the straits, through the bends, past the point, along the west end of town, past the green, the castle, the sea front, and beyond into . . . And then it's just burst.

. . . a patch of darkness that's congealed there, that's never gone away. And I'm heading straight for it. It's beckoning me. I'm crossing over towards it. Croeso, it says. Home.

Steph

At first I don't want to touch anything, which is difficult. I'm standing in my old room and I feel like Alice did when she ate the cake that made her big. I'm a giant. It's hard not to brush against the edge of the bed, my bed. It's still got the same duvet cover spread over it, the one my father chose, with the boats on it. I think he wanted me to be a sailor or something, an outdoorsy, Ellen Macarthur type, but these boats were enough for me. The only place I ever wanted to sail was straight to sleep, and I could back then. It was easy.

I avoid the bed and almost clatter into my wardrobe. There's a mirror on top and I'm slightly amazed my face still fits into it. But it's not so very different, I suppose: the eyes are less expectant and have lost a bit of blue (they say they do when you move away from the sea); the skin isn't quite as smooth; the cheekbones are a little submerged. Apart from that it's much the same. I'm not a sailor, but I'm no shipwreck either.

There's a sticker in the corner of the mirror, of a boy from a band, and I feel a bit sorry for him – trapped there all this time watching an empty room, abandoned and unadored, never allowed to get older. There must be thousands like him in vacated bedrooms all over the country, a legion of reluctant Peter Pans staring forlornly through the bars of their celluloid never-lands.

I don't want to touch anything because I'm afraid I'll mess

it up. God knows why, but my parents have left the room exactly as it was. It's as though they've preserved it. It's a bit eerie really, like it's a shrine or a room in a museum house, like it's a dead person's room. They've left my hairbrush on the bedside table and instinctively I go to pick it up but draw my hand back at the last second. What would happen if I pulled it through my living hair? I think there's a Miss Havisham lurking in all our mums and dads, keeping a place in cobwebs for us; and we're the betrayers, we're the deserters. Because I guess they always assumed I would come back, soon, for holidays, for Christmas, for them; and when I didn't they just carried on, carried on expecting me regardless, waited for their little girl to knock on the door and say I'm sorry.

'Come on, darling,' my mum shouts up the stairs, 'what's keeping you up there?'

And I'm wondering what's keeping me out of here. This is my room but it doesn't feel like it, not any more. If it was I'd be able to pick up that hairbrush, I'd be able to put my hands on everything, and instead I'm cringing my way around like a visitor in a plague ward.

You see, I think she might still be in here: the other Steph, the one I thought I'd left behind. Otherwise there'd be no need for this flinching, for maintaining these precious, withholding inches of quarantine. I can't even keep my face in the mirror for more than a second or two, in case I find her face in there, beside the boy in the band, staring spitefully back at me, wanting to come out, wanting to come back. I close my eyes but even that's not quite enough. I sense she's also spread herself more subtly about the room, has slyly perpetuated herself in invisible, mummified relics. And I'm worried they're still dormant, semi-alive, infectious; a pair of palsied hands reaching out from a coffin. Because try not to as we might, we're always trailing pieces of ourselves in our wakes, a scattering of breadcrumbs on the path, beckoning us back like crooked witches' fingers. And I can sense them in the air about me here, spores, seeds, germs, and I'm scared they might take root in me and grow into something terrible again, some abortive and misshapen flowering, some dark and horrible bloom. And that's the real truth I'm shrinking from: that I don't want to touch anything because I'm afraid it'll mess *me* up.

On the train I sat and read a paper. I could hear them droning out the names and feel the brakes contract against wheels. Prestatyn, Rhyl, Llandudno, Colwyn Bay. Stop and start, stop and start. The consonants rolling the call of my return. But I didn't risk looking up. I travelled through the news, home and international; through the editorials; through business. Nothing beyond the ink but paper. Conwy, Penmaenmawr, Llanfairfechan. Then a shadow crept in behind the print of the sports page and I knew it was there – that green expanse across the straits, that full stop in the sea that doesn't stop.

On the bus from Bangor I wore a mask. A set of features sculpted in alabaster; eyes immobile, averted; lips chiselled shut. Two old women crouched over on the seat in front of mine, shielding their bags of shopping from each other.

'*Mae'n hwyr*,' said the one.

'*Bob amser*,' said the other.

For an instant I feared they might turn around and recognize me, that they might stare and then startle and pucker their faces as if in the presence a ghost. But they didn't lift their eyes from their bags. Behind me two young boys watched bored as the bends snaked past through the windows. They were safely after my time.

And so things had carried on without me. Procreation. Birth. Ageing. The things we selfishly forget keep happening when we're gone, as though the places we leave behind become somehow sterile and static in our minds – sharks floating in formaldehyde, pictures painted on urns. Like the face that I'd brought back.

And which I brought right back – down Rosemary Lane, up Mount Street, on to Stanley Road, along the rows of toy-town houses – all the way to my front door. Where I stood for an age with my knuckles poised, ready to knock but not quite able to, as though my fist was like a wrecking ball about to smash through all the years I'd carefully erected between me and this door, as though propelling it those few more inches would bring all that time toppling down into a heap of dust and rubble. I might have turned and walked away but by then it was already too late, because the door had opened from the other side and there was no turning back. Watching my mother's face register confusion, doubt, disbelief, look down, look sideways, look up – and mine not moving, not an inch – before slowly it begins to dawn on her that this is real, that this is flesh and blood, her flesh and blood, and it's standing right in front of her eyes. Because look what the spring has brought her – my mother, who must have stopped believing a long while ago – an actual resurrection, an Easter miracle, a walking, breathing – though not talking, not yet, still not yet – Lazarus. And then, just as I have risen, she herself crumples to the ground; collapses in a heap there while I continue to stand stock-still above her, as motionless as an obelisk, gazing on like a stone god from another Easter altogether.

Afterwards the tears flow. Hers. My father's. Though I notice they're careful to blink them away every so often, to make sure their eyes haven't bleared over and deceived them. They watch me like hawks. They're loath to leave me out of their sight, even for a second. They keep touching me, letting their fingers linger against my arms. And I don't flinch, even though I don't like it. Because I understand they're afraid I'll disappear again, that I might evaporate and slip away from their grasp, that I might turn out to be the apparition they haven't quite, haven't absolutely, convinced themselves I'm not.

And for these first few hours they're careful to ask nothing of me, nothing at all. I'm swaddled in gossamer egg shells – a mayfly newly emerged, wings delicately gleaming, from its chrysalis. But I know that somewhere in the future some kind of explanation will be required (which isn't so much to ask, is it?), although for now they realize that they shouldn't question miracles, that they should accept this one on faith, learn to have faith in it, until I become not a miracle but their daughter once more. And then I guess I'll have to tell them. That I'm not really coming back for them. I'm coming back for her.

PART TWO

Town

Neil

There are a few places where the seasons don't come – deserts, equatorial islands, polar caps – and the George and Dragon is one of them. Outside I know it's spring. I've seen it this morning. The calendar confirms it: April, it says on top, and below a number six suckles on Miss KP Peanut's left breast, its little belly swelled with her salty milk. It's April 6th. It's one year into the new century. It's spring.

But inside here you'd never tell it. No equinox has ever intruded through these doors. They may have shone briefly through the glass of the windows, or splashed against them, or decorated them with patterns of frost, but they've never got in.

Two suns hang in the George's low, smoke-stained sky: the one in the east, above the bar; the other in the west, above a picture of the island – around whose shores its most famous wrecks perpetually flounder, their bows slanting down into the maw of a sea that has grimed over as it waits to swallow them. These suns radiate a weak, unvarying light through the room, which falls over the dimpled, copper surfaces of the tables and the smooth, faded cushions of the stools; which glimmers feebly off the brass bric-a-brac that covers the walls and casts shadows that never lengthen and never shrink.

There are other shadows too – only slightly more mobile – and these ones congregate about me at the bar, like spirits baying for the sacrificial blood that will allow them to speak.

I give them what I have, whole pints of it, and listen for their prophecies.

'Fucking hell, Neil, you been pissing in these pipes or what?' asks Billy Bins, as he has asked almost every day for years. It's not just the seasons that fail to change in this place.

'You know, I swear you've brought a touch of spring in with you today, Billy,' says Doctor Roger, slowly twisting his head as he speaks. He was a doctor once, although you'd be hard pressed to guess this past profession from his appearance now. I remember him in a prime of sorts, striding through the door of the clinic, knocking authoritatively on my infant knees and staring steadily and knowingly into the inflamed gulf of my throat. But like a leech bathed in salt he has contracted and shrivelled; his head is shrunken, Bornean, and his hands tremble like the wizened limbs of a tortoise feeling its way across scorched, Galapagosian plains.

'Aye, he's positively fragrant,' adds Dewi Tew, brushing a lank strand of his hair from his forehead, his bulk shuddering on his stool. 'Fresh like, glowing . . . what's the word I'm looking for, Doc?'

'Let me see now . . .' he says, mock-pondering, lifting the glass I've given him to his lips. Our roles have reversed these days: I have become the dispenser of his medicines, '. . . blooming, dewy . . .'

'Clean . . . new . . . sparkling . . .'.

'Yes, we're almost there . . . vernal . . . that's almost it . . . Yes, I've got it. Verdant!'

'Spot on, Doc!'

'Fuck off, the lot of you,' Billy spits glumly into to his beer. He's been on the back foot for about a year now – these exchanges are an endless chess game, advantages are pressed and weaknesses exploited, but on this chequerboard of mates there's never a Mate – ever since the waste collection company he works for changed its name, with an irony I truly believe they didn't intend, or even notice, to Verdant. They've painted it in huge letters on the side of Billy's lorry, so that each morning as it churns our rubbish it promises astounding and unfeasible transformations, an alchemy to turn our crap into rose petals, ordure into verdure. And compounding Billy's woes, they have made him wear a jacket of livid, almost luminescent, green, with the word emblazoned on the back.

It is fixed, at this very moment, to a hook on the black wooden beam that stands at the corner of the bar, where it dangles like the garish drapery of a dead tree, a counterfeit foliage glinting under the duplicate rays of false suns. For birdsong there is the metallic gurgling of the fruit machine which Billy feeds with stale pound coins. Dewi breathes Golden Virginian clouds into the sky, where for a second they seem almost blue. I watch them gather and thicken and dream of breezes that only blow in books, scented with draughts of the warm south, with oranges and lemons and spices. And I wonder how long I have breathed this air, this Dragon's air, which for all I know is the same air that was trapped inside when it was first built – in 1403, so the sign says – and has been recycled ever since, drawn through a thousand tarry lungs, absorbed into a million clotted arteries, exhaled past crooked legions of smoke-greyed teeth. There are histories and communities of breath, I suppose, which go far back and are not easily broken.

Seven years. That's how long. A drip in the Dragon's wheezing ocean. Almost a third of my life.

A lull has fallen. A minute's inadvertent silence to remember what they have all probably forgotten. Even the doctor, who touched her body that day, who took her wrist in his hand as they lifted her from where she lay among the fish-hooks and the buckets of gutted mackerel. Even Dewi, who stood watching on the pier, with his father's hand clamped on his wrist. Even Billy, who arrived an hour late and saw nothing but the empty beach and then came back here to tell everyone what he had seen.

A lull. A calm. A doldrums. Which can be just as deadly. There was no wind to speak of. The pressure high and rising. Northwest Fitzroy Sole Lundy Fastnet Irish Sea. Fair. Good. From St David's Head to Colwyn Bay.

Billy stares at scentless oranges and lemons and tries to nudge them into a winning sequence, to convert fool's gold into pennies, pictures of fruit into palpable harvests – and fails, as he has done a thousand times before. Doctor Roger examines the contents of his glass, which are flat and warm and yellow like urine in a test tube. Dewi's fingers are poised to tear the edges from a beer mat and I notice how his hands look old, even though he is younger than me. The ships off the island's shore keep their decks above the tobacco-blackened surface of the sea, while their motionless sails billow like insect wings caught in dirty amber.

The sky clear. Pellucid. Not a single cloud anywhere: not over the mountains, not over the Orme, not over the sea. Visibility perfect. Nothing stirring. The water like glass as far as you could see, from Traeth Lleiniog to Gallow's Point to the Penrhyn Docks. The sands, light-slicked and smooth; the sands, which in the other language are Wylofain, but were quiet that day, mute, when they should have cried out, when they should have screamed.

Seven years. Which is too long, perhaps. I was a promising child once, so people said, and promising children aren't meant to stay here. They're supposed to go away. They're supposed to make way for the old people, who creep into their abandoned nests like lizards. But sometimes things don't work out that way; sometimes you get a little stuck and all of a sudden people stop being surprised to see you still around, and you stop making up plans of flight to fob them off with. You become a fixture, like the brass trappings on these walls, and they forget quite what it was that you were meant to do. I'm the chick who grew up and never learnt to fly – who missed the exodus, the migration.

'You'll never guess who I saw this morning,' Billy says, reaching down to run his hand along the fruit machine's empty tray, a hopeful reflex that is almost never rewarded. Billy's world is full of the ends of rainbows, hidden pots of gold. I've seen him peek into the bins before he empties them. The others pause, as though they've not heard him, as though he's some mirage that's spun out of the machine. 'You'll never guess . . .' he begins again. But I don't need to guess. I already know.

They don't realize it but I've been waiting. Outside it is spring. I've seen it. It's April 6th. Thirteen years after, to the day. We've all come a long way.

Ricky

I'm not expecting much. Well, maybe a parade or something – my name on a banner hanging over the street, all the kids on the pavement waving flags, the mayor holding out a key for me. Ricky, my prodigal son, you'd best be having this. We've heard all about your great journeys and adventures. We've spent long hours recounting them; some people even turned them into songs and ballads. Subduing the natives in Acton. Plastering the great walls of Milton Keynes. Those brown-brick palaces you built in Surrey. Those silver shrines that rose beneath your hands in Hoxton. Those nights in the harems of Hamburg. You've come a long way, Ricky, and now it's time to honour your deeds.

And don't tell me you've never thought it, just for a bit, just for a second or two; never had – in your head before you go to sleep – an imaginary, triumphant homecoming.

Not that this is my home, not properly like. But the village is two miles away and you'd never muster a parade there; you'd have to make do with a fête, I reckon. And besides, this is as near as fuck to being home. I spent enough time here. The four of us. And only Steph a real town kid; the rest of us just hicks abroad in the mini-metropolis, dazzled by the pavements and the bigger Spar. The four of us, and towards the end me reckoning I'd be happier with the two of us. And then there was only three.

I'm not expecting much, and sure enough much isn't any-where in sight. Fuck all's come out to greet me instead.

I park the car on the West End, in front of the Georgian terrace, and I'm sure they've given the houses a lick of paint or five since I last saw them 'cause they're positively beam-ing today, glowing like, even though it's April and the sun isn't so strong yet. They've done them in rose-pink and lime-green and primrose-yellow, and other colours too, as if they wanted to turn all this stone and concrete into coral beds, to flip the world upside down and have the underwater colours on top, in the air. I don't get it with these seaside places – the way they chuck their slap on when hardly anyone below a hun-dred and ten wants to go to them any more, like some old bird plastering herself when she knows the best she's going to do is get groped by some pensioner at the bar. I mean, who do they think they're going to fool? Please, come here, we're such jolly folk we paint our houses happy colours. Please stay. Please fork out sixty quid for a night in a place that looks like a frigging rainbow on the outside but is still damp and grim and grey on the inside. A word to the wise: the brighter and more colourful these places look, the more fucking *desperate* they are.

I duck down behind them, behind the façade, on to Rose-mary Lane where Will Garage is smoking a fag by the empty pumps (why don't they just get rid of them? They've been jaffas since I was a kid). I could stop and say hello but he doesn't look up and so I pass by without saying anything. There'll be time for all that later. Well fuck, if it isn't Ricky. Long time no see. You owe me a tenner, mate. Ha ha! Slaps on the back all round. Plenty of time.

I reach the bakery on Margaret Street and turn up past the old gaol. They took us here on primary school trips – only two miles, but a trip's a trip I suppose – and showed us a treadmill and a gallows, though I'm not exactly sure what we were meant to learn by seeing them. Maybe it was some not too cunning lesson: you work and then you die. We were village kids, best not get our hopes up. Then I'm past the gaol and on the street in front of the doctor's surgery, wondering if Doctor Roger's liver has turned into a barrel of cider yet. And then I'm looking down at my feet wondering what the fuck they've done.

Because this isn't the way. Not the proper way. If it was I would have been in the George and Dragon already. This is a detour and I swear I never noticed till now I was taking it. And I know where it's taking me. Up Mount Street, on to Stanley Road, past three doors . . . until all the roads have ended and turned into border towns . . .

'We're supposed to meet them, Ricky,' she says.

And I know we are. We've got a plan. Today is the day. But she looks so good that I don't want to share her with them, not with anyone. I've got plans of my own.

'There's loads of time,' I lie.

'What do you mean loads?'

'I mean loads. It's not even twelve yet, is it?'

Clang goes the church bell. And then clang another eleven times, just to rub it in. It's not only twelve, it's five minutes past twelve.

You see, we're running on town time now and it's not quite right. I know this 'cause a year ago Mr Jones our teacher took us to the goal and the guide woman told us this story about the last man who was hung there; how he swears he's innocent, right up to the last, right up to the moment they're about to put the rope around his neck. And, just as they're going to, he points across to the clock on the church steeple and tells them he's putting a curse on it, that it'll never run on time again. And it didn't either, she tells us. It's been five minutes late ever since. Out of the corner of my eye I catch Mr Jones checking his watch with a frown. He's clearly appalled at the town's lateness, though probably not surprised. He's got that look in his eye that he gets when he's telling us about Babylon and Nineveh and Sodom and Gomorrah. The cities of the plain. The town by the sea. He's got grudges against them all. He's probably thinking that townsman deserved to get hung, even if he was innocent; and the town certainly deserved to get cursed, even if he was guilty. He's an unbelievable wanker is Mr Jones.

'Well, we've still got loads of time,' I say belligerently, the way you do when you know you're wrong.

It's just that I want her to stay here with me so much; here on this duvet with the boats floating across it, plunging in and out of the creases I've made trying to edge closer without her noticing. She's wearing this grey-black top with slightly puffy shoulders and I can see the outline of her bra straps and cups, little half-moons in a night mist, and I swear if she'd let me put my hands there I'd do anything for her, I'd jump right out the fucking window. Which I may have to do anyway if her mum knocks again; her mum, who's got so many airs and graces to her she's like a hurricane inside a cathedral.

'We're supposed to meet them at one,' she says.

I know, I know, I say in my head. But there's something in her voice that's saying maybe I've got a bit of leeway here, a space for negotiation. Not much, granted, but the way I'm reckoning there's only about twelve inches or so between us. I've not got far to go. I change tack and put a baffled, beaten-for-no-reason, puppy look on, which usually works, especially when you're a kid and you can really pull it off.

'It doesn't matter if we're a bit late, does it? They're not going to go without us.'

She's looking thoughtful now, with her legs pulled up in front of her and her elbows resting on her knees, twisting strands of her fringe between her fingers, trying to pull them into her mouth.

'I guess.'

Does this mean we can wait? Does this mean I can begin stealing another sly inch towards her? It would really help if I knew. This is so difficult. This has always been so difficult. Since the day Del tells us she's off to town to see her new mate, and Neil and me follow her, and she tells us to get lost, and we pretend we're going there anyway, and eventually it's settled that we're all going to town. And it turns out to be a bit of a jaunt like. We take the road as far as the old factory and then follow the beach behind the sea wall, picking various pieces of crap out of the seaweed as we go. Neil finds a dead tern and tries to take it with him, but Del makes him hide it till later. I find a strip of rubber from an inner tube or something and try flicking Neil with it, but Del gives me a kick in the shin. It's turning into a real day out. The funny thing's that we've been to town loads of times, but never this way and never alone. I've come in with my mum, shopping and that, but always on the bus or in a car. And it's the same for the others too, I can tell, 'cause we have to stop when we reach the headland just before the town and check if we can get around it. The road doesn't follow the shore here – it cuts right past towards the castle. The shore's our way and it's different. It's new. You know, sometimes it doesn't take much to make your world a little bigger and stranger; sometimes it only takes you going there on your own.

You can tell she's surprised when the three of us turn up on her doorstep. Del just gives her a nod and a look and doesn't bother with an explanation, like we're some disease she's picked up and can't get rid of, like we're part of the whole Del package and she can take it or leave it – Del's not going to be bothered either way. And she takes it, which is no surprise. None of us say no to Del, not in the end.

I don't remember what we did for the rest of that day. All I remember is standing in front of her door, not being able to look at her properly, feeling like I should be doing something but not knowing what. And for some reason I'm overcome with the overwhelming impulse to slap Neil on the back of the head, which I do – before I even know her name – and afterwards I don't even know why I've done it and I'm thinking that was a twatish thing to do, not because Neil didn't deserve it but because that's probably what she thinks. Because suddenly it was difficult. And it's still difficult. And there's no explaining it, honestly. One moment I'm showing Del and Tracy Evans my knob in the toilets at school, and they're letting me put my hand in their knickers, and it's all easy, it's all a bit of a laugh – a nervy, breathless one, I'll admit – and the next I'm here, needing a team from NASA to help me navigate my arm around Steph's shoulders.

'We don't have to go,' she says.

What? I think. I'm lost here. I'm sinking like the boats beneath my hands. I'm all at fucking sea – which is where we're supposed to be going, and which is where I didn't, not for a second, think we had the choice not to go. To be late, yes, but it's never even come into my head that we could not go at all. I mean, this is Del's plan, surely we can't dodge it altogether. But things are a bit weird between Steph and Del and I don't know why and I don't understand what's happening. I don't understand what the rules are any more, what we can and can't do.

'We'd better,' I say, and she looks over at me like Jesus didn't look at Judas, but probably wanted to.

'Well, let's go then,' she spits out, like I'm dragging her by the hair or something.

But it's not my fault, I want to say, it's not me. We've got a plan, we've got Del's plan. And it's a shit plan, I'm suddenly thinking. It's a fucking kid's plan. It's a shit plan and I knew it was. I knew it was.

I turn sharply down on to Steeple Lane. I've got to keep moving, I've got to stay on the roads. Because I don't want to be stuck here.

Steph

I best not keep them waiting. I can hear the church bells ringing. Oranges and lemons say the bells . . . but not these bells.
They say something else. They're saying it's twelve o'clock,
which means I'm already five minutes late.

But I'm not in a hurry. Without noticing it I've shrunk
back into my room; it seems to fit again. I hang my head out
the window, light a cigarette, and watch a thin finger of
smoke curl out and then stop, like it can't make up its mind,
attempt to curl back in again, and then founder as it tries to
grasp the sill. Over the slate of the rooftops an oily snow of
gull shit has fallen.

I wonder what they'll look like now. Down beneath me
Stanley Road is showing the years: its skin's a bit pitted, it's
creased around the pavements; it could do with a tar-lift
really, a bit of a nip and tuck. As I watch, Mrs Griffiths
totters past pushing a walker, or the walker totters past
pulling her – I can't be certain which. And I keep thinking
that maybe I'll see Ricky come around the corner, that
maybe he'll come here first. I mean, I know he'll come to
town, because I asked him to, but will he come here before
we're meant to meet? He would have once. He would have
stood below this window and thrown a pebble – he didn't like
to knock because he hated my mother, because she hated him
– and I liked it that he did, that I could make him do that
without asking. And let's be honest, we never want to give up

33

anything, ever, even if we've not had it for years; especially the knowing that we don't even have to ask.

Maybe he'll think it was me that found him, that looked him up; because in my letter I didn't mention that it wasn't me, that it was Neil, that this was all Neil's idea, Neil's plan. Poor Neil, who never left. Little Chicken Neil, whose sky was always falling. Cluck Cluck Thomas who always doubted and never dared.

From the very first time. When Del turned up on the doorstep, with the pair of them loitering behind her, twiddling their thumbs and saying nothing. Her two shadows: one twitchy and pale and nervous, the other dark and cocky and unaware that he's nervous. Neil and Ricky, whose names I don't know yet because Del just looks at me, flicks her head sideways, and says:

'We're going down the pier.'

As though it's her that's invited me here; me, who's standing on my own doorstep.

So, of course, we end up going to the pier. Del in front, pushing impatiently past the pensioners who line the pavement, gumming ice-creams and catching cancer from the sunbeams. Del leading the way, parting the tourist sea, with Neil and Ricky close behind in her wake; though Ricky has begun to loiter, I note, to fall back towards where I bring up the rear. We cross Castle Street and the cars seem to stop for Del, who doesn't bother looking left and right, which they teach us to do in my school – who knows what they teach them in the villages? And because it's summer all the shops have put out boxes full of kids' stuff, mini-cricket bats and tennis balls, little shrimp nets on bamboo poles – which I used to catch butterflies with – footballs made of thin plastic that are so light they swerve crazily when you kick them, and we all linger by them for a second or two, not long enough for the others to notice, we think; because secretly we'd like to pick something out and run off somewhere to play with it, because this new kind of playing that we have to do without them is harder and we don't quite know how it works yet, what the rules are.

On the front of the pier there's too many people. The old ones sit slumped on the benches; the parents eat chips and then smear oil on their white skins and try to fry. The air is seaside seasoned, with salt and sweat and coconut. Smaller children dangle crab-lines over the railings, baited with off-cuts from the butcher's tied in orange netted bags, which they lower between the girders into the swell. You can see the water rising and falling over these bundles of skin and fat and sinew, snapped below by crabs' claws and above by gulls' beaks. I see Neil watching them, transfixed, a kind of horror spreading through his pale eyes; he's clutching the railing so hard the blood's flowed out of his hands and his fingers look like guttered wax on the metal. Maybe the others see this too. Maybe one of them does, at least.

'Let's go to the launch,' says Ricky.

No, say Neil's eyes. No.

'All right,' says Del, and makes our decision with a step towards the pier's end.

At the end of the pier the tide has brought the water to the launch's edge; it rises, laps its sides, overflows them, and then is sucked back down with the retreating swell. It makes me think of breathing. It makes Neil think of not being able to breathe. He's trying not to look below, to keep his gaze safely in the oxygen of the horizon.

'To four,' says Ricky.

'Three,' says Del.

The rules are being made. The game is taking shape. There's an iron ladder fixed on the side of the pier that leads on to the launch; it has ten rungs which, as they descend, become slimier and greener where the sea has tried to climb them. What we have to do is get down this ladder, on to the far side of the launch, and stand there for three seconds – counted by the others, properly, with Mississippis – hoping we've timed it right and don't get a soaking, or worse, from the returning swell.

Ricky insists on going first. He makes it look easy, waiting on the second-to-last rung for the water to begin to recede (but not entirely finish receding, because that's the trick: to make your move while the water's still on its way out; to buy yourself one precious second with wet feet in order to escape a drenched pair of trousers, or being swept out into the sea) before dashing over to the side and standing there while Del tries to insert a few malicious pauses between the syllables – on the penultimate 'ss' he spots this and jumps back on to the second rung, just as the launch is submerged.

'That wasn't three!'

'Was!'

And we all know it was, so it's left at that. Del goes next and because she does her own counting there's never any doubt she's going to make it.

Neil's chest is ebbing and surging more than the water that terrifies him. His ribs rise and fall beneath his jumper like bits of flotsam on the tide. Here at the pier's end there are fewer people – some fishermen sat by their rods, a couple on a bench eating ice-creams, a man staring across at the mountains through the metal telescope that for ten pence enlarges the view – though surely the mountains are big enough on their own – and yet Neil is desperately searching their faces, as though he hopes they might see what is happening, that they might step in from the safety of their world and pull him out of his. But our game has made us separate, invisible, even though we occupy the same space. The telescope can't show them the pupils dilating in Neil's eyes, or the way his legs have begun to tremble.

'Neil's next, Neil's next,' Ricky chants.

Del looks over at me, but because I'm new I know I can be last if I want to – this time at least. And I do want to go last. I can't help it, but I want to see Neil go. And I want to see him fail too.

He stands at the top of the ladder while beneath him the water churns and seethes, heaving itself up on to the surface of the launch where it briefly writhes, wet and dark, like a knot of eels. He turns his back on it and lowers his foot on to the first rung, then the second, then stops for an age, his whole body gone rigor mortis stiff.

'Come on, Neil, get a fucking move on,' Ricky shouts, wanting him to get a soaking like he didn't, wanting to show me that he can do things that Neil can't.

'Go on,' Del says, almost in a whisper. And with a surprise I realize that she really wants him to make it, for him to get through this and for it to be OK. I don't say anything.

He gets to the fifth rung.

'You're almost there,' I hear her say, with a tenderness I never expected.

'Don't be such a frigging chicken!'

Then, from beneath the pier's edge, over which only the licks in his thin brown hair remain visible, comes his voice, low and whimpering:

'I can't, I can't.' As though a whole ocean is already slithering coldly through his lungs.

We go to the edge, look over, and find him embracing the ladder with his arms, his face pressed hard against its iron rungs. The whimpering has become a desperate gasping and gulping.

'You don't have to,' Del says. 'Come back up. It doesn't matter.'

'I can't, I can't.'

And then the gasping and gulping have joined together to

become one single sound, one wailing cry which I can't tell is an inhalation or an exhalation, a sound made of all the breath inside him or all the breath he can't get inside.

What I can tell for certain is that it's loud, startlingly loud, loud enough to travel right through into that other dimension where the fisherman now puts down his rod and the man takes his eye away from the mountains, where they both begin rushing towards us. I start to edge backwards, wanting to leave all this behind; not wanting them to discover me here in this game. They're getting closer and I'm trying to become a passer-by. But before I've got far enough away they've arrived. And because I've been watching them I haven't seen that Del's already pulled Neil back on to the pier, that he's standing with her arm draped lightly around his shoulder, his head inclined slightly towards hers (where he wants to rest it, where he wants to hide), and even Ricky hangs solicitously by his side (in the briefest of half-seconds he brushes his hand against Neil's elbow). The men ask some questions. The others answer them. But I know without hearing that they've re-established their separateness. They've closed ranks. And I notice then that I'm outside them. From the very first time.

Neil

Ricky arrives first. He comes barging through the door as though he'd just popped out for a bit to buy cigarettes. A few shards of sunlight manage to sneak in behind him and he seems to carry them along in his wake; the brass on the walls glints, the copper on the tables flickers, the shades around the bar blink their eyes and move their tongues and throng about him. They all speak at once to begin with and you can tell he's trying to hold them at bay. And then he looks past them and sees me. He winks and smiles.

I wait for the rest of them to drink their fill of him. He tells them some stories, laughs at their jokes as if he'd not heard them, throws names of places into the air and juggles them there, makes them spin and scintillate like planets, gives them new worlds to look at without having to leave their seats. He's better than newspapers, almost as good as TV. And I remember this Ricky so well. Ricky Ryan, pretending to be everyone's mate; Ricky Ryan, my best mate.

I wait and watch, knowing that in here at least there's no hurry; that in here time doesn't eddy and flow – it hardly moves, it's called. Ricky swivels on his stool, punctuates his punch-lines with a flourish of his hands, scrunches his face in amazement, shock, horror, amusement, outrage, or any other expression he needs to shape it into. Doc nods his head, Dewi laughs out loud, Billy tries to keep up and join in but can't. Ricky's too quick. He's a natural, a one-man show. And seeing him perform I remember how afterwards he stopped all the teasing and taunting and smoothed the way for me, carried me; let me be his straight man, his shadow. How in the big school he clowned so I wouldn't be noticed, let the older lads bait him so I wouldn't get caught. How he tried to make things easier. Like I want him to make them easier now.

I can't quite believe he's back in town. I'd like to reach over the bar with my hand and make sure. But I know he's real. Sometimes it's the town I worry about.

In primary school our teacher Mr Jones used to tell us about towns and villages that had been drowned. There were the ancient ones that the sea had got, leaving their church bells to chime beneath the waves. And then there were the ones the English had done for; damming rivers and filling up valleys to quench their voracious thirsts. Llanwddyn, Capel Celyn – he'd call them out, his voice hard with outrage, as though he could see their dry tongues edging closer, panting over the rim of the hills. In class I sat and wondered where all the people who lived in them had gone, and later, in my nightmares, I began to sense the waters rising; over the stones on Penmon beach, up the cliffs at Caim, over the banks of the river Lleiniog, through the doors and windows of our houses, across our roofs, until the village was just a ripple on their surface and the hills around us were islands; until I knew where the people had gone because I was one of them, my lungs straining in agony, my fingers held out to catch the last bubbles of breath that had escaped them, my eyeballs bulging upwards towards the deluged sky. On waking I'd rush to the window of my room to gulp in the morning and make sure that it was still made of air.

But for hours after some residue of these nightmares would linger. Even on the sunniest of days a certain dampness seemed to cling to the surface of things, a dankness beyond mere dew. At breakfast my father's skin would appear unnaturally clammy and maggoty-white. There would be a kind of sliminess coating my own skin, making me worry that at any moment the handle of my teacup might slip out of my hands. And I couldn't get it out of my head that perhaps my nightmare had been true and we were actually wandering about in a sodden aftermath, caught in some post-diluvian delusion in which we were unaware that we had already drowned. Later on I'd walk through the village, averting my eyes from the people who called out to me, feeling like the last man in that film about the body-snatchers – the only one who knew.

When I moved to town I thought I could leave these dreams behind me and set my feet on higher, more solid ground. I remember how at some point Ricky and me both began to cling to the town; how we'd get off the school bus here together even though it meant walking the extra miles home – we kept to the roads then, when once upon a time we would have followed the shore. Until, first chance we got, we moved here. And then, the first chance he got, Ricky moved on, and kept moving. At the time I didn't mind. I didn't blame him. He wanted a future and I was happy just to have a present, with my feet firmly fixed on the dry land of the George and Dragon.

Somewhere out in space, between the earth and the sun, there's a place called the Lagrangion Point. It's the juncture at which the gravity of these two bodies is cancelled out and any object left there will not move, not ever. That's where I'd like to live. There'd be no tides, or seasons: nothing would fall, nothing would rise, nothing would sink. Because lately, as I've made my way along the town's pavements, they've not felt as solid as they should. I see walls tremble and surfaces dissolve. I see things I shouldn't see. There's some kind of terrible gravity at work here, and it's pulling her back.

Ricky's speaking to me gently, quietly, so the others won't hear.

'She's not here yet,' he says.

And what I want to tell him is: 'Ricky, I see her everywhere, all the time. And I don't want to any more. I don't want to. I can't live with her coming back like this. I can't, I can't.'

Ricky

I've been in here all of five seconds and they're at it already. Doctor Roger starts things off.

'It's been a while, Ricky.'

It has, Doc. Long enough for your liver to have packed its bags and moved into the pickle jar it's due to retire into. Fuck Spain, Doc, you're ending up in vinegar, pal.

'Been about have we, Ricky?'

Go on, say it. Like your dad, Ricky. Like your pikey dad. Who couldn't keep his feet and his knob in one place for the time it took dust to settle, let alone for you to grow up. And honestly, right now I'm proud of my dad, wherever he is, 'cause he's not wearing out a stool with his arse like these lot. Doc, Billy, Dewi – I mean, Christ, if there was an earthquake this frigging minute they'd be the last things in town left sitting.

Pikey, gyppo, tinker. It's not like I've not heard it all a thousand times before – in school, in the village, in town. Ricky Nig, 'cause my skin's a bit dark like. It's the Irish in me, you see, the black Irish. My dad was swarthy as a Spaniard. I've seen a picture of him, and I swear he looked just like a pirate. You'd think my mother's side would've balanced things out a bit, with their copper-tops and see-through, freckly skin, but wouldn't that be typical of my old man's genes, to get everywhere? No, I'm so used to this shit I just fall back into the old routine, humour the fuckers, act all matey, bring a ray of light into their sad little lives – and God knows they need it, it's dark as an arsehole in here.

Neil's hovering in the background. He's trying to blend in with the optics; which isn't that hard seeing he's still so pale he's almost transparent. He's always had this way of not quite being there, if you know what I mean. Even when we were kids there were times you'd lose sight of him. It'd be like 'Where's Neil?', and he'd be right beside you, but somehow he'd have slipped out of view, gone invisible for a minute or two. I give him a wink, just to let him know I'm biding my time with this lot, giving them their dues, and then we can say hello properly like.

Not that we need to. It's funny, but once you've known someone for ages, like really ages, the hello bit's pointless. If you've spent that much time together, the other time you've not spent together doesn't seem to count. I mean, the second you meet it's like it doesn't exist, like it didn't happen. And when you try to describe it it's as if you're telling a story about someone else. Which can be a bit of a pisser. When I think of all the shit I've been up to the last five years and suddenly I'm here in the George again and it's like I only nipped out for a leak.

Still, these others are lapping it up. I'm on a roll now, laying it on thick, making myself out like some kind of Sinbad come back from the high seas. And suddenly I'm thinking of how people used to say that that was what my dad was like, that he could've yarned for Wales, only I never heard him 'cause he wasn't there. I remember his mum though, my nain, and she was just the same. She lived in this tiny caravan, in a field outside the village, and I'd go there all the time after school. She'd fill me up with sweets, till I was buzzing on sugar, and tell me about travelling to the fairs with her mum and dad. They were those country fairs they used to have, the ones where they brought pigs and horses to sell and the farmer boys could have the day off to get pissed and batter each other. They were big events apparently, regular carnivals, and my nain'd get dead excited and chortle and chuckle as she spoke about them, as though she was getting kitted out to go to one and not to spend the night running after the leaks in her roof with a bowl.

You see, they weren't just about selling animals: there was a whole package that went with them. Of course the horses were the main show, and they'd start the day with a parade of them, done up with ribbons and stuff in their manes. But after that there was all sorts going on. They'd have freak shows, with bearded ladies and dwarves and a strong man, and this one huge fat fucker they called Johnny Bach. There were coconut shies, stalls selling Pwllheli rock, a family of travelling boxers from Somerset, even a tent where this bird dressed up as a genie took her top off – which must have been a hell of a thrill for some of them farmer lads, who didn't get many chances to see a pair of tits that weren't for milking. And this is where my nain's mum comes in, because she was the one with Llewelyn, the dancing bear.

He wasn't the only thing they brought around with them – my nain's dad sold harnesses and bridles and loads of gear that'd fallen off the back of vans – or carts back then, I suppose – but he was pretty successful apparently. They had a special tent for him, with pine trees and hills and honeycombs painted on the inside, and when it was full they'd bring Llew in on his lead and my great-grandmother would clap her hands and he'd start to dance. My nain tried to show me his dance once. It looked like one of them the Russians do, arms crossed, legs kicking, though maybe she was better at it than Llew, or worse. But the crowds couldn't get enough of it, she said. They'd clap along, getting faster, and he'd follow their beat and speed up.

They went all over the place with that bear and his twinkle-paws. From fair to fair, across the island, down the mainland coast, right into the South and the valleys. He must have been famous. My nain says she loved the life: the packing up, the setting up, the farmers who waved at them on the roads, the old ladies who came with cakes for Llew. And she loved the others who travelled with them. The strong man let her sit on his shoulders, she'd help trim the bearded lady, play hide and seek with the dwarves, hose down Johnny Bach when it got too filthy between the folds in his belly. They were good people, she said. Proud people, like she was. And they must have loved that bear too, because when he died they gave him a proper burial, in a field by Menai Bridge. He had a real coffin and everything, made specially. On the day of the funeral the strong man carried it to the hole, followed by a procession of the fair lot, and quite a few locals too. Can you believe it! A funeral for a fucking bear. But Llew was special, my nain said. He must have been, because after he died they kept one of his claws and embossed it with gold. And I'll let you into a little secret: I've got that claw. My nain gave it to me, and it's hanging from a chain around my neck.

I'm on a roll and Billy only has to go and spoil things. I'm in the middle of some story and he has to go and say it: 'You're a chip off the old block you are, Ricky.' Billy, who knows I never knew him. Billy, who looks like he's wearing fucking foliage, letting me know that he knows the pikey roots I've branched from. And I'm thinking fuck you, I'd prefer to be with them fair bunch than you lot. I'm thinking I'm sick of entertaining these wankers, who laugh down their noses at my jokes, reckoning they're better than me 'cause their ancestors only fucked each other. And I could carry on the banter but suddenly I've had enough, I've had a frigging bellyful of this. I'm not going to dance for them. I'm not going to dance for them any more.

I wish Steph was here. I wish Del was here too. I wish that more than anything.

Steph

On Stanley Road the houses look like they've been built by elves. They're so small, running up the hill towards the woods and fields like they know they should be getting back there, like they know they're really cottages and cottages shouldn't live in towns.

Of course down on Castle Street and the sea front they're bigger. Brighter too. The hotels and the guest-houses, the shops, the castle. But that's this town all over really – all show, all front. It's like some hulking theatrical set, built by little people who creep off at night to hide behind it. Ricky told me once that his teacher in primary school taught them that the English built the whole town; it was only a village to begin with, and when they came they chucked everyone out and herded them off to some place right on the other side of the island. Then they moved in and started putting up their castles and tea-shops. And sometimes, when I was a kid, I'd get this strange feeling that I wasn't supposed to be here, that these other people were still around, peering at me reproachfully with their ghost eyes from behind the walls, staring down from the woods on the top of the hill, wandering the streets in the darkness and gathering in the children who hadn't – like me – been allowed to grow up in the town.

It was easier for my mother. She knew she wasn't supposed to be here. It was her *terrible mistake*. You could always tell when she was going to say it. Usually it was midway through an argument with my dad, when she'd start breaking up her sentences with sobs, and then out it would slip: 'This . . . this has been . . . a . . . a terrible mistake.'

And my dad was always stupid enough to ask: 'What has?'

'This has!' she'd blurt out, indicating with her hands what appeared to be the room she was standing in but was actually everything outside of it: our house, my dad's shop, the town, the island, the people who lived on it. The people whom she had to serve while inwardly she cringed, imagining that other life she might have lived, the one in which she hadn't met my dad and let him take her away from her parents' leafy street in Richmond to some seaside relic in another West, a West that by rights should've been nothing more than the memory of a childhood holiday.

Sometimes, when we were alone together, she'd give me this pitying look, and I knew the *terrible mistake* was lurking behind it. Only this time it was me who was its victim. Because in her mind it had cut me off from the life that I should have lived too, the same one that she'd had growing up. And she did her best to redeem me from this error, sending me to schools that no one else from the town went to, keeping me off the streets where everyone else played, letting me know at every opportunity that I was different because eighteen years ago she'd hung out in Covent Garden and known how to use the Underground.

On Steeple Lane it's as though nobody sees me. I walk along the pavement and they cast blank eyes in my direction before passing silently by. There's a group of old women gathered around the entrance to the post office, where they nod and coo like pigeons, the crumbs of their pensions clamped firmly in their pockets. Mrs Griffiths is in the centre, with her long fingers wrapped around the spongy black grips of her walker's handles. She used to hold my wrists like that; clutching them while with her other hand she placed my fingers on the keys. Relax, she'd say, you can't play with talons. And now she's clasping her walker like an eagle. I'm sure she looks up when I go past but there's not even a flicker of recognition on her face. It's easy to become a stranger.

All Good Boys Deserve Fun. That's what she used to tell me. The gaps were a FACE. I'd try to memorize this while I sat waiting for my lesson in her kitchen, beside an Aga that she never turned down, even in the summer, and which smelt like corned beef and polish. All Good Boys . . . which must have meant Mr Griffiths wasn't that good, because he was always sitting in the kitchen looking like being married to Mrs Griffiths wasn't any fun at all. My dad said she used to be a nun before she met Mr Griffiths and started teaching piano. She had two moles on her chin with long black hairs growing out of them, and sometimes, when she leant over to place my fingers on the keys, I'd worry that they were going to tickle the back of my neck.

He used to show me these books full of pictures of Roman mosaics as I waited. He collected them, I guess, and us pupils were a captive audience. There were lots of people dressed in togas and tunics, columns, bunches of grapes everywhere. In some pictures there were soldiers, with rectangular shields and short swords, and in others there were gardens with walls draped in vines, where girls dressed loosely in white cotton, with flowers in their hair, danced in unmoving, ceramic circles. He lingered over these longer than the others, his eyes as glazed and still as their clay bodies, lacquered mementoes of a long-forgotten heat.

I dawdle outside the butcher's and Mr Williams comes out the door in his bloodied apron and mistakes me for a piece of meat. I sense his eyes weighing up my breasts and thighs, the fleshy curve of my buttocks, the soft tissue of my neck. He can't see me. He can't see the little girl whose father sent her here on Thursdays to buy lamb chops and sausages.

'And so what'll it be, Stephie bach?'

'Chops and sausages please, Mr Williams.'

'Well, let's just see what we can find for Stephie then. Look, here's a leg of lamb.'

'But my dad said chops and sausages.'

'Did he now, cariad? Not a joint of beef? – I've got one here, you know.'

'He said chops and sausages, Mr Williams.'

'Well then, chops and sausages it'll have to be then, Stephie. I can't disappoint my favourite customer, can I?'

And now I'm just a woman on the street.

It's easy to become a stranger: all you have to do is run away. That's what I wanted to tell my mother when I first saw her. Not sorry, but look, it's so easy. To run. To go. Except that when you do there's no stopping. It's like jumping off a merry-go-round when you were a kid – the motion stays inside you, spinning through your head and body in nauseous revolutions.

With the George and Dragon's sign in sight I make a detour. I slip down Little Lane, past the Catholic church, and head towards the castle. The pink of cherry blossom flickers through the gates of the old rectory and I remember that we were supposed to bring flowers to take with us. Roses, Neil said. Wild roses. But where are you supposed to find wild roses in April? And why should it matter what kind?

Beyond the castle walls there are nothing but fields and woods. This is where the town ends. These walls used to be covered in ivy, my father told me. When he was a kid it cascaded over the ramparts and turrets, falling almost to the ground, and made the castle look like a huge piece of shrubbery, or some lost temple overgrown by an avenging jungle. And then one day they tore it off, wrenched its centipede's feet from the rock, and made the walls stand naked and defiant again, letting the fields and woods and everything beyond know that they couldn't come back, not yet, not now.

I walk from the castle to the sea front and the promenade, where the old people have settled on the benches, surrounded by gulls who greedily eye the sandwiches that tremble in their hands. They sit in silence mostly, staring out towards the sea. When I was younger I used to wonder why they came this far to look at water. All those hours spent cramped in overheated coaches, trapped in traffic, winding perilously along narrow roads and lanes. And for what? To take one cursory glance at the castle, to buy some worthless souvenir from my father's shop, and then to rest their gaze on the empty surface of the straits.

I used to think that all water was the same. But it isn't. And that's why we have to go, why we have to go again To my right I can see our route, along the promenade, across the green, around the headland, and then through the woods and fields until we reach another shore, off which another island sits. And it doesn't look so far away, but it is. It's thirteen years away and none of us have reached it yet.

Ricky

You should see the state of them when she comes in. Dewi pulling his greasy fringe down over his forehead to hide the high-tide mark of his hairline. Billy trying to play it cool, fumbling with the coins in his pocket, and ending up looking like he's playing with himself. The Doctor pretending he doesn't even notice, giving himself heartburn by gulping his cider (he's moved on to halves now – it's what alkies drink to stretch out the day). And let's be fair, she's not looking half bad.

It's only Neil that doesn't gawp. He's getting himself ready to go and being silly careful about it, lacing up a pair of walking boots, unfolding this green raincoat he's put behind the bar – there's not a sodding cloud in the sky – with one eye on the clock behind the Smirnoff bottle and the other God knows where. He's been off with the fairies ever since I arrived. I've hardly got a proper sentence out of him.

She sees me first and I'm dead glad about it. Honestly, she's beautiful. And I'm trying to work out if she's more beautiful now than she was before, and then I'm worrying if it makes me a bit of a perv just remembering someone when they were that young. I haven't seen her since we were fifteen. I haven't touched her since we were twelve.

The others don't even know who she is. I'd like to tell them right now, just to sour the drool in their gobs for a second. That's Steph Edwards you're leering over, I'd like to say.

Don't you remember? John's little girl, John from Castle Gifts. Don't you remember her, Doc, sitting in your office with her arm bared for your needle? Come on, Billy, the one in the blue uniform, getting into her mum's car to go to school. Don't you remember the pictures? Have you seen this girl? Because that's what they asked: the pictures her dad had printed when she did her runner. They were plastered all over the town, over all the towns, from here to Rhyl. Steph's face and shoulders, wearing her school blazer and tie, staring off lamp-posts and out of chip-shop windows, lit up by the glow of arcade games, smiling at you in phone booths. And I knew it wasn't right but there was a part of me that was pissed off about the whole thing, because there's me been trying to put her to the back of my head and suddenly I can't go fucking anywhere without seeing her. Her dad even comes up to me on the street and gives me one of the pictures, in case I haven't already seen a hundred of them. And for a few years I kept it. Only for a few, mind.

She sees me first, and I know it's stupid but I can feel that little jump your stomach makes, that jolt, like there's this bubble of air in there that's broken loose and it's trying to rise up into your chest. It's mad how your body remembers stuff even when you think you don't. It's like there's all these feelings hibernating in your nerves and suddenly they crawl yawning out into the light of day. I saw this nature programme once, where they dug up a fish from the bottom of a dried-up lake; there hadn't been a drop of water in it for years, and the fish was just a clump of earth, but when they chipped the earth off and put the thing in a tank it started swimming around as though it'd never stopped swimming, as though it hadn't spent a single second with dirt stuffed in its gills.

I go to meet her halfway, so we can talk without the others hearing. Because they'll only make a song and dance about it if they find out who she is. There's not too many dramas in the George and they'd go to town on this one. Missing girl returns. It's a bigger piece of soap than's ever been in Billy's hands.

'A-right, Steph,' I say. And fuck it all if I haven't started smiling.

'Hi there, Ricky,' she says, and maybe there's a grin in there somewhere but I'm not seeing it.

So tell me, what are you supposed to say? What kind of small talk is big enough? We could chat about what we're going to do, about where we're going, but all that seems so strange I've not even allowed myself to think about it properly yet.

'Are you going to get me a drink or what then, Ricky?' Yes, the grin's there now, definitely. The voice is a bit rougher, I notice. Not the one she got from her mum.

'If there's time,' I say, nodding over towards Neil – who's still fumbling with some crap behind the bar – as if the sight of him will explain everything and make us standing here less awkward.

But it's not as awkward as I'd thought it'd be. This isn't as difficult as I'd expected. It's easier. She's had her hair cut shorter. I think she's taller. It's like I don't know her at all. It's like we've just met in some random pub, in some random place, and decided to go for a stroll together. It's only my body that remembers. The smoothness. The softness of skin long shed.

'Maybe we'd best be off,' I say, feeling them lot's eyes trying to creep around my shoulders to take a gander.

And then we're out on Castle Street, the three of us, walking in silence towards the promenade with the seagulls yawping and screeching above our heads. It's one of those delicate spring days, the ones with skies like them blue egg shells, and if it weren't for the gulls swooping about it'd be perfectly still and calm. You should see Neil flinching from the fuckers, when they get a bit close like, as if they're pterodactyls or something. Neil, kitted out in his raincoat and boots, with a bag hanging off his back, like we're off on an expedition to the ends of the frigging earth. Steph's two steps ahead of us on the street, she's really motoring. And I'm a bit worried she might knock over this group of pensioners a coach has just dropped off on the pavement; they're doddering about, dead slow, zombie-style, staring through the Spar window like it's some great historical monument, and Steph seems like she's in a hell of a hurry. She's not looking at anything. Nothing. Not even her dad's shop – it's only on the other side of the street. I mean, fair dos, she's not exactly wasting time. She's not been here for ten years and she doesn't even bother taking a peek down memory lane.

Her steps don't slow until we reach the promenade. Then she begins to lag. Maybe we're all lagging a bit. It takes us an age to get across the green. I've been practising about ten conversations in my mind, but every time I look ahead and see where we're going they don't seem like the right ones. It's as though if I were to open my mouth the weirdness of us being here together, the weirdness of what we're doing, would come seeping out. It's like for now we have to keep Del out of this and pretend we just happened to meet, and happened to go for a wander, and that wander will happen to take us to the very place.

When we reach the end of the green Steph's last. There's a gate leading away from the town on to the headland and into the fields, and it's Neil who reaches it first and opens it. It's Neil who's leading the way now.

PART THREE

The Monkey Woods

Neil

I don't normally come this far, not these days. If I'm walking on my own I'll circle from the George to the pier and then back again. But here I am at the gate. On my right I can see the shore curving around the headland, then down into Fryars Bay, before trailing away behind the point. On my left the fields roll up Baron Hill and disappear into the trees; the trees that for now remain a sere remnant, winter brown – apart from at their far edge, where the monkey woods grow, dark and evergreen. The mansion is hidden behind their branches, and the gatehouse too, where the Candyman used to live. My father's house is out of sight, in the village.

For me this view will always be the wrong way round; a reflection in a mirror, a landscape in reverse. Because before we met Steph we always came from over there. It was simple. We headed for the town. You learn to see in one direction and it's hard to stop and change trajectories, to make backwards become forwards, to turn where you've been into where you're going.

Steph and Ricky watch me as I open the gate. Or rather, Ricky is watching Steph, who's watching me. Normally I was always the last, but not today. I doubt Steph even remembers the way. She'll have to follow me. And Ricky always followed her.

Steph

'Let's go down to the Candyman's,' says Del.

'But it's late,' I say.

'No it isn't,' she says. And she's right. The sun is still high above the straits. It'll be hours before it bloodies the sky over Baron Hill.

'Come on,' she says, 'I'm bored.' She swivels an impatient toe in the pebbles of the beach. The town and the sea front have suddenly lost their lustre. There are two kids fishing for crabs off the pier and their lines sway listlessly in the afternoon swell. Behind us Mrs Griffiths's dog is running in pointless circles on the green. We're both bored. But I'm less adventurous and bold. I'm tentative, nervy, a little bit frightened – of there, of him.

'Come on,' she says, and eventually I do. This is how it works: she has plans and I follow them. I follow her. This is how it's always worked, ever since last year when her mother first brought her into my father's shop. Her striding out in front, pulling a magazine off the shelf and belligerently opening it; me sheltering behind my father, lifting an agitated finger to my lips. And it should have been the other way around. Even then it is obvious. This is my place. This belongs to my father. Her mother has just begun working for *us*. But it isn't.

Over the green we go, over the grassy headland that sits on the edge of town and slowly tumbles into the sea, stranding trees and shrubs in the water. We follow the shore for half a mile, passing hidden dens and hangouts. There's the derelict hulk of the old lifeboat house, where the older boys come to smoke and drink and write their names; where Ricky found a magazine once, full of naked women leaning forward on their hands and knees and stretching open the cleft of their buttocks; where Neil found a condom under a beer can and didn't know what it was. Beyond it there's a kind of grotto, made of stones piled on top of each other, with a driftwood roof, where the younger children shelter and camp, huddled in a damp and claustrophobic freedom. There are others like these all about the purlieus of the town – tree houses, abandoned sheds, ruined cottages – a whole shanty suburbia where its children commute to grow up. But within ten minutes we have left them behind and entered the countryside proper. My town has meagre limits and you can overrun them with one mad dash, in a blink of the eye. This is farmland. This is village territory. This is my terra incognita. Where Del lives. And where he lives too.

We drift inland, away from the shore, following lanes that twist and turn and shrink. Thorny branches tangle up the horizon. Brambles and nettles reach out to grab me. I dodge them and flinch. But Del is at home. She tomboys down the lane, swishing a stick like a machete, and I follow her as though she were a woodchopper in a fairy tale.

And I wouldn't mind this so much if back in the town our roles were reversed; if it were my heels she chased, if she were to stop every now and again, lost in some bumpkin confusion, and turn to me for guidance. But it's never like that. She strides around the place like she owns it. She discovers things I didn't even see. She banters with the boys who try to tease her. I don't think she even notices the girls who don't talk to her. So for now I've given up on place as a means of switching places and am holding out for time to do my work – to erect one boundary that she won't slip so effortlessly over.

You see, I know I'm pretty. And I know she's not. I mean, look at her. There's a podgy quiver of fat all over her that I'm guessing will prove far more resilient than a puppy's. Sometimes when she skips she wobbles like a seal. Then there's her glasses, with their thick frames of translucent pink and scratched lenses, out of which her eyes peer, small, confident, piggy, entirely blind to the social curse they look through. She wears farmer's clothes: lumpy, knitted sweaters the colour of mud; cast-off jeans that are too big for her in the wrong way; a pair of old, nameless trainers. Her mother cuts her hair. It makes me a little sad – she's my best friend, for now – but also a bit proud and a lot relieved. Because I know these things and she doesn't. It's my secret resource, my hidden consolation as I bide my time. And already there have been intimations that the world we are moving towards favours me. The boys she banters with tie up their tongues in front of me and start hitting each other or stealing car aerials. The girls who ignore her have begun to keep me in the corner of their watchful, suspicious stares. I'm waiting to arrive, to get there ahead. I'm about to.

But we aren't there yet, not yet. We're going to the Candyman's cottage. And she's leading the way.

Along lanes that grow narrower and hedges that grow taller, that rise and arch and cut away the comforting sight of the sea. It has dwindled to a smell now, a familiar hint of salt that seasons a host of other more exotic and unsavoury scents, which Del identifies and lists with a connoisseur's smugness:

'That's pig shit . . . chicken shit . . .'

As if I care. Manure is all just shit. Full stop. I want to turn back and watch television – the children's stuff in the afternoon, where there's streets and concrete and not a cow-pat in sight. But I'm not sure how to get home. I'm probably two miles from my front door and I doubt I could find my way there on my own.

I should keep an eye out for markers. I should pay more attention. I should scatter a trail of memories behind me. But one tree looks like another, the crossroads have no signs, and though the squat cottages that nestle around them have names carved in slate by their doors I haven't bothered reading them. Del keeps up her commentary.

'That's Mrs Evans's place. She's a bitch. My mum hates her.'

'Robert Mong lives there. He's twenty-five and he pisses in his pants. Really, he does!'

'Mr Thomas thinks his wife's still alive. I've heard him talking to her.'

Which is very well and good but is hardly a map out of here: when I next see these cottages they'll all look the same and might as well have all these people sitting inside together, around a table, with a wet patch beneath Robert's chair, and Mr Thomas nattering to a ghost while Mrs Evans slags her off.

Eventually Del's voice becomes a background sound, like the birdsong from the trees and bushes whose names I don't know, sung by birds I couldn't tell apart. The scenery has turned into a repetitive sequence – hedge, cottage, gate, view of field, view of another hedge on its far side, view of the field behind it, cows, hedge – a rustic merry-go-round that left to my own devices I would circle endlessly. I stick closer to Del, making sure to keep beyond the arc of her perpetually swishing stick.

'Don't mind them,' Del says. 'They won't bother us.'

I hear every syllable of this. The merry-go-round has stopped and left me standing in the bottom corner of a wide, sloping field. A herd of cows have sprung to life on its far side and are beginning to lumber towards us. Their hooves throw up clumps of mud, the same mud my own feet are frozen in. I should never have climbed over the gate. I should never have left the safety of the lane. I shouldn't be here.

'Why are they running then?'

'Just keep walking.'

'I'm not moving, Del. Forget it, let's go back.'

'Don't be a baby. We're almost there.'

'We're not!'

'We are. The monkey woods are right there.'

'Fuck off. I'm not moving.'

But they are. They're galloping now – if that's what they call it for cows – they're bucking and jumping and charging and kicking their back legs into the air. They're not behaving like cows are supposed to – not the ones who sit around and chew their cud in the field beside the green anyway – no, it's like they've just burst into a rodeo ring with invisible cowboys on their backs. Panic twists my stomach. The mud takes a firmer hold of my shoes. Some cruel optical prank stretches the space between me and the gate into a million hopeless miles. I'm trying to get words out of my mouth but the single pathetic one I can manage is 'Del', uttered in a whimpering, wheedling croak like a toddler in the dark calling for its mother. And all I want her to say is they won't come near you, they won't hurt you, like a mum would say, don't worry, there's nothing living under your bed. But she doesn't. She says, 'Run.' And for a second I'm astounded, flabbergasted, like all the assuaging, assuring authority has suddenly vanished out of the world, like the mum's just said, 'Fuck, so there is a monster under there!'

And then I run.

And run. Which is a miracle. Because although my legs are pumping below my waist it seems to be through no volition of my own; they feel weak, weightless, without substance, a tingling mush of flesh wrapped around the rubbery hollows that were once my bones. Yet I appear to be moving. Or at least the ground is moving. It's hard to tell which. This feels like the fleeing sprint in a nightmare, the dream velocity that doesn't get you anywhere, let alone away, but I can see the distance in front of me contracting and the wall that Del is clambering over is getting unmistakably closer. And then with no consciousness of having even reached it I'm over it too. Everything is still. Everything is calm. In a moment of sharp and absolute clarity I look up and see a raven floating serenely over me in the sky. It's like nothing's happened. It's like I've woken up to find my sheets tangled around my sweating limbs.

'See, told you not to worry!' she says.

If I had the energy I'd shout, but I don't, so instead I laugh. We both do. We've reached the monkey woods.

Ricky

It's so well hidden behind the trees that you'd never find it if you didn't know it was there. You can't see it from anywhere, not until it's right in front of your face. Which is mad really 'cause it's massive, so massive you'd think a few trees wouldn't make a blind bit of difference, wouldn't hide one wing of it let alone the whole thing.

We've not come far inland but already the straits and the shore seem a long way behind us. They're only three wide fields away but they look miles and miles off, like they're a picture on a brochure for somewhere else, like you'd have to fly there for a holiday. Islands make everything seem bigger. One yard here is the same as ten over there on the mainland, I'm telling you. When I was growing up this was like an entire compacted country: a quick stroll and you'd have done the hills, the plains, the sea, the lot. But I reckon that also makes islands the opposite. They make everything seem smaller too. Which would explain why the old mansion can hide behind a few trees.

It's amazing how fast things fall down. I've not been here for ten years, tops, and it doesn't take long to notice the two front columns gone horizontal on to the grass; the big staircase collapsed halfway up, stranding the upper storeys; the extra slates that have vanished; the floorboards that have become ragged stumps against the walls, splintered reminders of rooms. I used to know every inch of this place, where it was safe to stand, where the timbers were still solid, but the second I step inside it today I realize I wouldn't have a clue now – a few more steps forward and I'd end up breaking my neck.

The others won't even come in this far. Steph's standing by the stables, near the entrance to the drive, which is so overgrown it's almost a tunnel. Neil's staring up at the crumpled railings of the balcony as if he's expecting some lords and ladies to walk out on to it and throw him a penny. They're both eager to be off but I want a few more minutes, just to look.

You see, I used to think he might live here. My dad. I know it sounds absolutely fucking stupid, but I did. When I was seven I heard my mum talking to a neighbour about how she remembered when the Poles lived in the mansion during the war, because they couldn't go home. And I didn't really know what a Pole was, except that Joe the Baker – who came around the village in his van selling bread – was one, and I didn't really know why the Poles couldn't go home, or where their homes were. But I must've got it into my thick skull that people who couldn't go home must live in the mansion, and I definitely knew that my dad couldn't come home. My mum would've carved him up with a butcher's knife before he wiped his feet on the mat. You're never too young to know that.

And so one day I set off to find it, all on my tod, all on my lonesome, without a frigging clue where I was headed. I mean, a mansion, it couldn't be so hard to spot, could it? Little Ricky Nig, with nothing but a Twix melting in his pocket and a mansion, a stranger and a bunch of Poles in his head, off into the wild green yonder. Nain and Llew would've been proud as hell of me.

But maybe not so proud two hours later, when I'm walking in circles through the monkey woods, lost as fuck, dizzy lost, blubbering like a fucking faucet; seeing the monkey-puzzle trees as huge as skyscrapers and then as tiny as toadstools; seeing cottages grow gables and columns and balconies and then turn back into cottages; and me not even close yet, not even knowing where I'm supposed to be getting close to, whether the circles I'm spinning in are taking me nearer or further.

Outside the door Neil and Steph are waiting for me. But I want a few more minutes. I want to look. Outside the door everything is bigger and smaller.

Neil

'Come up here, Neil. Come on.' She's already on the balcony, leaning against railings that I sense are about to topple. Come down, Del, is what I want to say; we'll be safer on the ground. But she's not afraid of anything.

'Follow Ricky, he knows the way up!'

But I'm not sure he does any more. He's standing a few feet within the doorway, looking like he doesn't know which way to go. When I passed by the door I could see how the staircase had collapsed, how the floorboards had fallen through, how the slates and rafters had gone. It's different now, Del, I want to tell her, it's changed. Things have broken and we can't go the same way.

But still she beckons, fearless, leaning against those railings that I fear will topple beneath her weight. Except that then I realize they will not topple because she has no weight to press against them any more.

Steph

Del and I catch our breath and creep on through the monkey woods. I remember the first time they took me here. They thought that because they were different they were exciting and mysterious. They came here all the time, and the day they first brought me I could sense the anticipation welling up in them, the fidgety thrill of letting someone in on a secret. Ricky almost pushed me over the wall. Neil started flitting between the tree trunks. Del stood out in front, watching me from behind the reflective sheen of her lenses, waiting. They were all waiting. And for what? For me to look around in wonder at a bunch of trees that didn't lose their leaves in the winter. I looked up at the canopy above me and said nothing. Neil stopped moving. The stick in Del's hand went still. Obviously, like some blinkered explorer, I was standing among marvels I couldn't see.

'They're monkey-puzzle trees,' said Ricky from behind me in a prompting whisper.

'What are?'

'They are,' said Del, pointing at the same canopy I was looking at.

Amongst the lighter green of the pine needles I began to make out the dark, tubular shapes of other boughs.

'You know, like them toy things,' Ricky urged.

'What toys?'

'You know, them things where you hang monkeys off each other by the arms. Neil's got one.'

'I do,' said Neil.

'Oh, them,' I lied. I didn't want to disappoint everyone.

'Look like them, don't they?'

'Yeh, they do.' And they do. About five years ago I saw one for the first time in the back of a charity shop; a pole with pegs running down its sides – like a miniature coat-rack – off which dangled a troupe of plastic monkeys, balanced arm in interlocking arm. I was with a friend and when I saw it I pointed in excitement and said, 'Look, it's a monkey puzzle. Like the tree!' And she looked at it blankly for a second or two. 'Oh, right. So it is,' she lied.

There was something unnatural about them – if nature means by chance – a crafted symmetry that seemed more the product of a mould than a seed. Its needles were thick and waxy; its branches were a sweep of carefully constellated cat's tails.

'He had them planted,' said Del.

'He did,' said Neil. 'They're from China.'

'My mum says they're African,' said Ricky.

'Don't be stupid, they're too green for Africa,' said Del.

'Africa's green. It's got jungles an' all sorts.'

'S'not green on telly, is it? It's deserts and sand now 'cause of the draught.'

'Is green.'

'Not now.'

'Well, it was.'

'Well, they're not from there anyway. They're from Japan.'

'China,' Neil interjected.

'Same thing,' said Del.

'They're not,' Neil gasped. 'They're not the same. Japan invaded China. I . . . I . . . I know that. I know that.'

'Shut up, Neil.'

'Who?' I asked, and they all looked around at me, grateful to have someone about whose ignorance was universal.

'Who what?' said Del.

'Who had them planted?'

'The Candyman,' they replied.

With Del today, beneath the woods' evergreen canopies and ever-damp shades, the sounds of the outer world have become distorted and strange. The soft, feathered cooing of a pigeon is a parrot's manic squawk; the lowing of the cattle the plaintive baying of a wolf pack; the short, catarrhy croaks of the crows have amplified into a primate chatter, a din of whoops and howls and hollers that aren't Jungle-Book friendly but somehow vicious and demented. Cat's tails have become tarantula legs, poking out from the recesses of dark caves, caressing the air in search of us.

But Del doesn't flinch. Not once. She brushes them nonchalantly aside and allows me to cower in her protective wake. And as we make our way towards the drive that leads down from the ruined mansion, I begin to realize that I think I love her – this girl in her too big cast-offs with saucer-bottoms for eyes. I realize how thankful I am that she can take me here and make me feel safe, that she can live so fearlessly in this world of monsters. I sense that ache of gratitude that I think is love. And maybe it is. Maybe it's the simple thanks we give for protection.

If she would let me I would like to hold her hand.

'Come in,' he says.

They made out like they discovered him, living out here alone in the old gatehouse; the gatehouse with no gate, guarding a mansion that no one has lived in for half a century or more. Their own bogeyman in their special woods. And because he's their own he turns out to be not quite as bad as you'd expect. He gives them Mars bars and KitKats when they visit. Sometimes he lets the boys share a can of lager. He tells them stories about the mansion, which he says belongs to him. They believe anything he says: that he stitched together this Frankenstein's forest; that his family were all Sirs once and owned the whole island; that everything has gone to rot since then, spoiled by the tasteless parvenus who flocked here on the roads that his forefathers had built. The present is a tacky nightmare and he can't wake up.

'The Candyman planted them,' they'd said.

But how could that be possible, I'd thought, when they first took me to him? He was old, yes, but as old as the trees under which he lurked?

'Come in,' he says, ushering us towards the door. 'Come in, come in.' His voice isn't like our voices. It sounds like a radio voice. It sounds like the voice my mum uses when we have visitors. As he speaks he smiles and thick jowls bulge out beneath his jaw; the skin the colour of a raw chicken's, with erratic patches of ashy stubble poking through it. Salt and pepper feathers, half-plucked. He holds the door open and behind him I can see a painting hanging on a wall, of a girl in a light-blue dress trapped in an ornate garden, holding a pink parasol. She looks unhappily out at me from beneath its shadow. I don't want to go in. But Del has already bolted over the threshold.

Inside it is too warm, much too warm. Outside it was just right. Spring is almost here and the air was comfortable. He's made us sit by the kitchen table, on big chairs with cushions made of wool, or something equally scratchy and hot. Del squirms and fidgets on hers, rubbing her thighs together to assuage the itchiness. I see him watching and keep mine dead still. My mother has told me.

'Well then,' says the Candyman, peering down from

where he stands by the cupboard, 'so what can I get for my visitors?'

His eyes are trying hard to look kind, so hard they squint. The irises are as pale and moist as salamanders' bellies. I want the sun to be in here but the only window is covered in a white blind, which smothers its comforting light. 'Biscuits, some chocolate?' He reaches into the cupboard to pull out a box and there's something about the way he moves, about the quick, considered uncrooking of his elbow, the carefulness of his fingers, that makes me think of snakes' tongues. I can see Del's hand twitch impatiently on her lap, waiting for gifts. If only she would let me I would hold it.

Ricky

He's still not there. He wasn't there the first time either. After I'd knackered myself out careering around those frigging woods I'd come to a clearing, with a house in the middle. It was painted white and had roses and stuff growing up the walls – none of the pebble-dash shit we had all over our place. It had this short wall around it and a garden, with more flowers, and this man was snipping them with a pair of shears. I came to a stop near the wall 'cause I thought maybe this was the mansion (how was I supposed to know what they looked like, or how big they should be, or if there was only one type of them?) and maybe this was one of them Poles – I knew it wasn't my dad 'cause he was dark like me and this bloke was as white as an egg from a factory hen. And I've been standing there for a bit, yeh, only a bit, when I notice he's looking at me, and I'm about to move on but before I do he's walked over to the wall and started talking to me.

'Can I help you, young man?'

Young man? Nobody calls kids 'young man' – except the doctor, I guess. And his voice sounds like the doctor's too – when he's in the clinic anyway – soft and proper and concerned like. He's dressed a bit the same as well, with a jacket and shirt – just to cut some flowers in his garden! And the young Ryan generator's working overtime trying to take this in and sort it out, and I'm standing there in gormless silence with him waiting, all fucking patience, until at last I blurt it out.

'Is this the mansion?'

'I'm sorry, young man, but this is just the gatehouse. The mansion's up the drive.'

He's wearing this straw hat with a ribbon round it. I've never seen anybody round here wearing one of them, apart from those blokes who turn up in the town for regattas and that.

'Might I ask what you're looking for up there?'

Might I ask? Christ!

'Nothing!'

'Well, it must be something, mustn't it?'

'S'nothing!'

So now I know I'm close and all I've got to do is ditch this bloke and get there. But he's turning out to be a real persistent bastard.

'Would you like a drink or something? I think I've got some lemonade in the house.'

I don't want lemonade. I want to get to the mansion.

'I'm a-right.'

It's becoming a stand-off. Why he's trying to be so sodding nice is beyond me. Maybe it's a Pole thing. But I'm not backing down, not when I'm this close, and eventually he goes into the house saying he's got something for me there, and I scarper up the drive. I can tell he's watching me do it too, through the window, but I don't give a shit to be honest. He can watch me all he fucking likes.

I should know there's nobody there just from the drive. The rhododendron bushes have pinched it into a path; fallen trees have made it an obstacle course. The only footprints in the gravel are cloven.

From the outside I can't tell whether it's bigger or smaller then I imagined. On the inside it's a whole lot emptier though. I'd reckoned on furniture and carpets and curtains, but there's nothing but graffiti on the walls and fresh air in the windows. I walk from room to room and it's like there's no end of them; it's like I could walk for ever and keep on finding new rooms. Occasionally there's a crisp packet or a Coke can on the floor and I pick them up, all hopeful like, because if there's rubbish there's people; you can't have rubbish without people. Somebody's been here. These pieces of crap are clues and if only I could follow them. And I'm trying to but there's so many rooms. But what if they run out, I'm suddenly thinking, what if I reach the last one and there's nobody? And then it's me who's run out, right out the door, and I'm on the drive, running and running.

Steph

Neil's walking towards the entrance to the drive. He brushes past the fronds of young ferns to where the boughs of the trees mesh and thicken into arches. Beneath them the shadows fall together into darkness, a darkness that has more mass than the spring light and swallows it. It swallows Neil too. He's so skinny. He's as thin as the light. When I looked at him on the street in his green anorak it was as though he was billowing along on an invisible clothes-line, an outline of cloth swelled meagrely with air.

Ricky's still got his head in the door, searching with his eyes through the wreckage inside the mansion. 'Ricky,' I call. 'Ricky.' A pair of crows startle at my voice and rise momentarily over the tops of the trees, the sun igniting the blackness of their feathers. I know he'll come when he hears me.

Neil has vanished. He's become the quiver and rustle of rhododendron leaves. I would have thought he'd be afraid of the dark, like he used to be afraid of everything else, but as I follow him down the drive I realize that it's me who's afraid of this dark. Still. Except that this time I've brought my own light. Reaching into my jeans pocket, I feel for its reassurance: the smooth plastic, the tiny, skin-clasping serrations of the flint wheel.

Neil

Del was his favourite. Ricky and me he tolerated, I suppose, because we always came along. But it was Del he really wanted to see.

'Come in, come in,' he'd say.

He called us young men and women and we were only kids.

I'd heard my father call him a relic. Sir Bad Old Days he'd joke, when he was talking to his friends in the village and I was hiding behind his legs. He'd owned my taid's farm once, and nobody liked landlords back then apparently, especially ones that spoke English in Eton accents. But we didn't care.

It was Ricky who found him. He'd been sneaking off somewhere when he thought Del and I weren't looking. So one day we followed him. He ran up through the village, through the woods, past the gatehouse and into the mansion. We kept out of sight and watched as he went from room to room, stooping now and then to pick up the pieces of rubbish that other invading children had left behind; he'd hold them in his hand and scrutinize them, as though he were an archaeologist picking his way through a tomb, or staring at its walls trying to read the hieroglyphics. Then he came out and ran down the drive, and we ran after him, and when we came to the gatehouse the Candyman was waiting in his garden.

'Come in, come in,' he said.

I remember the furniture inside. It was too big for the cottage. A chaise longue crowded the corridor behind the door and there was barely enough room to squeeze past it; the walls tottered up to the low ceilings under the burden of heavy gilded frames, in which gardens and parks lay cramped and dead people were coffined. A huge glass chandelier hung lustreless in the gloom of the sitting room, like a peacock stuffed into a cage. Even the tables and chairs in the kitchen chafed against the corners of the room, as though they were bodies pinched into clothes that didn't fit.

He always had something to give us. Out of the cupboard would come boxes of boiled sweets, biscuits, chocolates – which he must have bought in readiness, just in case we happened to come by. I suppose he must have been lonely, but at that age you don't even suspect that old people can be lonely. They don't have to stand in the corner of the school yard, watching the games the others play. He lived safely on his own, and when you're a child loneliness is other children – not the people you can't see but the ones you can't be with.

He always had something. And in return all we had to do was listen. They sounded like stories from the old novels Miss Roberts would read us in school when Mr Jones wasn't around. How Sir John Bulkelton fought a duel with pistols on the sands of the straits; how Lady Sarah Bulkelton was taken tragically young by tuberculosis, wasting away among lavender fumes and cold handkerchiefs; there were faithful hounds and garden parties, visits from dukes, ancestors who rode with Wellington at Waterloo. And maybe he realized that to us they would only sound like stories, because after a while he started bringing out papers and letters and diaries, reading them reverently to us as though each word would reassure us of their reality, would spread out before us in the cramped kitchen of his cottage the whole wide tapestry of his past. But somehow, while he read, my father's words would come back to me. And I'd begin to hear voices that weren't on the pages, or were hidden away in their margins, voices that hated these people, that didn't want them here, but which lingered just beyond the Candyman's hearing. And they'd get muddled in my mind with the gurgled cries of the drowned people, calling out in bubbles of breath, and I'd think in amazement how the island could hold all these voices at once without them hearing each other.

But Del was the one he wanted to hear most. And see too. As though through his stories he could conjure himself into one of the young Sirs his words described, not their dwindled remnant; that he could piece back together his estates in her eyes, make her see them into existence again. Because of all of us she was the least interested, the most confidently unimpressed. She draped herself over the hulking limbs of his chairs, sprawled insouciant in their wooden fists, bored, distracted, only waiting for what he would give us. You see, Del never liked cobwebs, or the spiders who tried to spin them. And eventually he must have realized that. Because later it was Steph he wanted to see most,

Ricky

The gatehouse is empty too now. The Candyman carked it years back, is what I heard, and I can't say I shed oceans when I did hear it. I mean, 'young man' and all that other shit, for fuck's sake. What was he like! Stuffed in that cottage with all them pictures and papers. And a stuffed dog too . . . almost forgotten that. A stuffed spaniel or something, sitting by his fireplace, with a stuffed pheasant shoved in his stuffed gob. There's a bunch of weird ones around this island. Take a step or two off the road and you'll find a whole world of liquorice allsorts. Still, he was only a harmless old fucker I suppose.

Steph had to climb over a bunch of fallen trees to get down the drive and my body was remembering like crazy, I'm telling you. I couldn't help it, I swear. And I tried to spark up some lame conversation like 'So . . . what you been up to this decade?' but honestly, it would've taken a flame-thrower or something to get it lit. Steph was having none of it. Her face was set hard as hell, like yesterday's concrete, and if a word of my moidering was breaking through then I couldn't tell.

When we arrived it was in pretty good shape. Some kids had smashed the windows and everything, but the door and roof were still intact – usually it's the slates that get nicked first round here, which always baffles me a bit 'cause there's great mountainfuls of them over the straits. Which reminds me of the day our school took us to see the mines at Blaenau Ffestiniog and Neil screamed when we went down into the pit . . . but that's another story. Anyway, Steph's looking through one of the windows, and Neil's moping in the garden – it's all brambles now, not a flower in sight – when it occurs to me that that stuffed dog might still be in there, and what the fuck, I think, why not have a peek? It'd be funny to see it again. Maybe take it back with me, as a bit of a pub novelty thing. So I give the door a kick and it swings straight open.

They've made a hell of a state of it. The papers and books and crap they've just ripped up and chucked on the floor. But the paintings, well, they've drawn all sorts on them – moustaches on the posh birds, cocks on the old fellers, and then some trippy magic mushroom nonsense on the landscape stuff: swirls and circles and weird scrawls of pigs. Someone's written 'I am the lord of the pigs' below one of them. Magies – you forget how much they do your head in. Wouldn't touch them these days. I've got enough bad thoughts spinning round my head without sending them for a twirl on that set of Waltzers. Scream if you want to go faster, the man at the fair used to shout. And I'd be screaming all right. To get off.

I get to the living room and I already know there's no chance that dog's still there. A load of fucked kids, a stuffed spaniel with a bird in its gob – it's not going to end well for the dog, is it? Or the bird. And they've done a real number on the living room too, turned it into a right little den of iniquity. There's a mattress been pulled down from upstairs and it's oilier than used goods from a porn set. There's old johnnies lying everywhere, like shoals of beached jellyfish, and scatterings of spliff butts toed into the mouldy carpet. And I'm thinking I'm going to catch a frigging dose just from standing here, there's probably a crustacean army marching up my legs right now, so I back out into the corridor and head towards the door. I can hear Steph rummaging around in the kitchen but I don't look what's she's doing there 'cause I need some fresh air. I really do.

Steph

The air has become unbreathably warm. It can't get in and it can't get out. I try to breathe it but it's sticky, like the strands of caramel that hang from the edges of Del's lips. Behind her I can see his hands which are snakes' tongues, flicking and lapping the too warm air.

He's talking but I can't hear him. Neither can Del. She bites through the surface of the chocolate and the caramel keeps oozing out on to her lips. She tries to wipe it away but instead smears it across her cheek. I try to lean forward to wipe it away but the arms of my chair seem to be holding me down. But Del's stood up. She moves impatiently across the kitchen, not listening to his words, and stops for a while to look at a portrait of a grey man in a black suit, whose eyes look pale and moist as though the paint were fading and still wet at the same time. She reaches over to touch it and then he's behind her, with his fingers burrowed weakly into the cloth that covers her shoulder, lying limp and cold there like dying lugworms in the sand.

'Get off,' she says. And brushes them away as though they were spiders.

He retracts them and I go to get up but the chair won't let me. I've found a gap at the edge of the white blind and I can see the walls of the garden and the yellow dust of the path. And I find if I look hard enough then it's like my feet are moving across it, back to the drive and the monkey trees and fields, back on to the green where Mrs Griffiths's dog will still be running in circles, back across the streets to my living room where on television there are no fields and woods and cottages. But I don't know my own way back. I have to follow Del. And she's already on the path. I can see her hand clasped around the knotted wood of her stick. If only she would let me I would hold it. If only she would let me. But when I reach out the glass stops my fingers. And it's only then that I realize that she's left me here. Del, who's never left Ricky or Neil behind, anywhere, never. She's left me here. And then I realize I will not wake up from this.

Neil

Del's hiding behind the tree trunks. She's flickering around them like candlelight. I wish she wouldn't play hide and seek like this.

Ricky

Steph's torched the gatehouse. Would you fucking believe it! I'm outside for all of five minutes and I start smelling smoke, and I'm thinking, who'd be burning leaves this time of year? But this isn't wood smoke. It's got that tar and chemicals and creosote smell that old carpets give off; it's got that heaviness to it, the kind that keeps it low to the ground to begin with. And when I look around it turns out I'm right, 'cause it's hardly got up to the window yet, it's only just spilling over the sill, this slow, muffled, puke-yellow smoke that, when it's out, heads right back down towards the ground like it's knackered itself just getting out the window. But I've seen house fires before and I know it'll be having a second wind soon enough. And then I remember Steph.

By the time I get to the doorway she's already standing in it, with her back to me, looking in. And I know then that it was her who started it. Because she's looking back to make sure it's good and started. And there's no fucking need to really, 'cause the second wind's in full blow now, it's whooshing out through the windows and it's picked up some flames on its way, little pale orange fingers that clutch at the window sill, and then bigger gouts of it, great dragon's belches of the stuff that that poor fucker on the sign in Prestatyn could only have dreamed of. I grab hold of Steph to drag her away from the door and she doesn't stop me, but her eyes never leave the building, not for a second. She staring at it, and there's such a fury in that stare that I swear if the flames weren't doing the job her eyes'd do it for them.

So you've got to picture this scene. There's me holding Steph in the garden, with my arm around her shoulders (it's taken it ten years but it's got there), and Neil standing over by the edge of the woods, peering into them like he's not noticed the frigging blaze behind his back, and the smoke getting all lively now and sprinting up so high into the sky that there can't be a person this side of the Urals who can't see it. And I'm reckoning, whatever the fuck's going on here – and I've not got a clue, not a mouse's tit of one – it seems like it's only me who realizes this isn't some jape in the woods. This is arson. And there's a spark or two lighting up somewhere in my brain too, 'cause it occurs to me that I'm stuck in the forest with two lunatics and an inferno and every fire engine from here to Holyhead on its way. And it's arson. This is fucking arson. We've really got to get going.

But when I try to drag Steph away it's like the concrete her face is made of begins to crack and crumple; it looks jutted and jagged and painful, like a road splintering in an earthquake. I'm telling her, Steph, we've really got to go, we've really got to get a move on, and suddenly her mouth rips open and she starts screaming – loud, loud like you've never heard.

'You fucker,' she screams. 'You fucker.'

It's like her whole body's become the earthquake. I can hardly keep hold of her.

'You fucker,' she screams. And for a second I think she might be screaming at me. But it's not me. She's screaming at the cottage. And there's no one in it.

We've got to keep moving, I think. We've really got to.

PART FOUR

The Village

Neil

From the top of the hill you can see the smoke coming from my father's chimney, a straggling, unpunctuated, Indian sentence of it. There's smoke coming out of the other chimneys too, the staggered line of them that go down the roofs of the terraces that flank the street. Behind us the column rising up from the Candyman's cottage swells in the sky and dwarfs them all, making them look like spores cast by a giant mushroom.

Gruff Glo is outside the post office, holding his paper, waiting to gossip with anyone who comes in or out. He doesn't need the paper to get his news. If I was closer I'd be able to see the grey beneath the skin on his hands; the grains of coal dust safely sedimented there, beyond the reach of water. Down by the bridge Jack Cucu, whose father went to the war in Burma with my taid, is sitting on a bench looking into the river. Reverend Morris is talking to Mrs Evans outside Spar, trying to look interested, but his boredom is apparent in the impatient shuffling of his feet, in the sly, sideways glances he makes towards the horizon. I've known them for ever and yet they look strange to me today, vaguely tremulous, as though they were figures floating in an ornamental globe and if I was to walk closer I'd bump against a wall of invisible glass.

'Come on, Neil mate,' Ricky says from behind me, 'let's keep shifting here, all right? Let's get on the frigging road before anyone sees us.'

We've run most of the way from the Candyman's and he's breathing heavily and sweating. He comes up beside me and we head towards a broken section in the fence. Steph's a bit further behind, moving at her own pace. Most of the way here he held back to make sure she was following us.

'Christ almighty!' Ricky says when we're on the road. 'What the fuck was all that about? I mean, honestly, what the fuck was all that about?'

He swivels his head around, to check if Steph's made it to the fence, and then speaks to me, almost in a whisper.

'I mean, what's with her, Neil? That was fucking loopy. That was loony tunes, mate.'

Steph's come out on to the road. She stops and brushes her hands down her sides, slowly and deliberately, removing the twigs and pine needles that have stuck to her coat. She seems to shudder slightly at her own touch.

'I mean . . .'

But what he means is that he doesn't care. Steph could have burnt the whole island to the ground and he still wouldn't care. He'd take her side and make sure she made it with us. With some people time doesn't matter – you remember them in reflex, in a contraction of sinew. And everything you have become in the interval apart is like the severed head of a biologist's frog, leaving what you have been forever kicking and twitching on the laboratory table.

We wait for Steph to join us on the road and then walk down the hill into the village.

Ricky

The moment my feet touch the street is the moment I know why I got shot of this place to begin with. There's the same old fellers standing around outside Spar and the post office; there's the same old pebbles clinging to the walls of the houses; there's the same new kids sitting in the bus shelter, staring into their phones, not waiting for buses. But everyone's waiting for something and I remember this feeling clear as crystal: everyone's waiting for something and they don't know what it is and it's never going to happen, it's never going to turn up. There's village life for you. It's like you've retired before you've even got started. Sod school and that, they should just give you your pension book when you're born and have done with it.

Neil's not speaking and I'm thinking how for our first years in school he couldn't speak. Not that he was mute or anything; it was just he had this stammer thing, couldn't stop biting into his words, so his sentences came out like sawdust from a wood chipper. It was as if he was afraid of letting them out, as if he'd pluck up the courage to get half of one out, or a few letters maybe, and then bottle it. It wasn't a pretty sight, I'm telling you. His face'd go all red, his jaw would start jerking up and down like a fish's when it's out of water, and his stomach and chest would heave as though there was a good chance his breakfast would come out before the words did. And sometimes it did too.

It was dead awkward and weird. And I'm not proud of this, all right, but I kept my distance from him like everyone else. I mean, it's not easy trying to chat with someone who you know's going to have an epi when they try to answer you. And shit, there's a bit of your head back then that thinks you might catch the thing yourself, just from some stray drop of spit. And then there's the whole loser-by-association crap as well. So I'm not proud, yeh . . . but there it is.

The worst thing's that there's only thirty of us in the school anyway. We're a small flock so the weird sheep stands out that bit more, same as the black one: it's not got far to wander, nowhere to keep out of sight. Everyone knows everyone. And we know without it having to be said that's Neil's different because his mum's died, just like Gwynfor who lives on the end of the street blubs in Spar all the time 'cause he went to the Falklands. But we don't know any of this stuff in a proper logical way. I mean, there'll be Gwynfor standing beside the magazine rack with tears streaming down his face and a pendulum of snot swaying from the end of his nose, and Mrs Evans will look over all sympathetically like and then whisper to Mrs Thomas across the frozen goods section, 'Poor Gwynfor. It was the Falklands, you know,' and Mrs Thomas will nod back, 'Yes, the Falklands,' as though that explains everything, as if it's blindingly obvious, as if there's some unwritten law of the universe that says if you happened to go to the Falklands then a few years later you were going to end up snivelling in the aisle of a Spar. So we all knew why, but none of us knew *why*. What's a dead mum got to do with speaking? I don't have a dad and it doesn't make my tongue do spazzy cartwheels in my mouth. And the teachers and stuff don't make it any better. They treat him different but they don't treat him different enough.

We've got this rule, right, that every time you need to go to the bog you have to hold up your hand and ask, and you'd think it'd be frigging obvious that Neil's going to have a problem and a half with this. But do they let him off, do they just let him just slip off and do his business? Do they fuck!

The first few times it's agony for the lot of us. His hand poking slowly up and then:

'O . . . o . . . os . . . g . . . wel . . . wel . . . wel . . . w . . .'

It's excruciating. Between every syllable there's this massive, painful silence, and it feels like the end of the sentence is an eternity away and you're being stretched out on it like one of them torture things.

'w . . . ww . . . wch . . . y y y y y y y . . . yn . . .'

And honestly, you don't even want to laugh or nothing, you just want to go up to the poor bastard and stick your hand into his lungs and drag the fucking words out for him.

'. . . dd . . . dd . . . dd . . . dda . . .'

And you're thinking, why don't they stop this? It doesn't matter to them. It isn't important. And maybe some of the teachers would've but Mr Jones didn't allow exceptions: he made everyone do it. And for him it was important because it was in Welsh, just to show we had it or were getting it, and so Neil – who did have it! – was no exception. But Mr Jones didn't get it. Didn't fucking get that this wasn't about language. It was about speaking, which was so much more important. It was about speaking, not language, and he couldn't tell the fucking difference.

After a while Neil gave up trying. You'd see him waiting and waiting, shifting about on the little plastic bowl-shaped chairs we had, the piss swelling up in his guts, aching in his abdomen, until in the end it was easier to let it out instead of the words. He'd go still then and the smell would spread around him, and you knew that pool of piss was burning into him, hot and shameful and awful, burning right into his pale face which went blotchy and red. Then when everyone had made enough gagging, snorting sounds one of the teachers would come over and take him out of the room and we'd all be left looking at the pool on his chair, like it was lying on the bottom of a moon crater or something.

When he came back in he'd be wearing the pair of brown nylon trousers they kept in the cupboard in case of 'emergencies'. He'd have to wear them all day. Stuck in the corner of the school yard with this brown shiny beacon wrapped around his skinny legs, in case anyone'd forgot. And everyone avoiding him – including me, I'm not proud – apart from the ones who bother to run around him holding their noses: 'Nice kecs, Neil. Ha ha. Neil's pissed himself, Neil's pissed himself. Ho ho ho. Hee hee hee.' Everyone except Del. One day, just before the bell goes to call us back from break, she walks right on up to him and grabs his hand and walks towards the door, looking bold and defiant at the rest of us through her specs, like if she didn't give a shit about the brown trousers and the pissing and the stuttering then none of us could either. And then things got a little better. The words got easier. All of them.

Steph

We all know it but none of us say it. Del's house is at the bottom of the hill.

It's planted on the end of a terrace and looks as if it's holding all the other houses in place, that if you were to take it away then the rest of them would crash down the hill like dominoes. There's smoke coming out of the chimneys and it hangs in the air, softening the sunbeams, leaving everything suffused in that gauzy flashback light you get in films. There's a river beyond it, a bridge, a pebble-dashed bus shelter, a pub that doesn't want you coming inside, a chapel that nobody goes to, a church that nobody went to. The light's misleading: this isn't before – it's always. Nothing has changed. This is the village where Del lived.

The first time I came here was the first time I ate baked beans on toast and fish fingers. Every now and again in the shop Del's mum would suggest to my mum that I come over for the evening. And my mum would smile and say of course, what a good idea. Sometimes she'd lie more effusively and suggest a night. And then one day she must have lied even more effusively than usual – it was hard concealing the terrible mistake all the time, and easy to overdo the camouflage – because when I came home from school I caught my parents arguing about me going.

'Mair's expecting her,' my dad was saying in exasperation. 'I can't see what the problem is.'

But I never found out what the problem was because when I walked into the room my mum went silent. The terrible mistake was becoming something she had to keep hidden from me as well.

Del's mum dished up at the counter while I drank orange squash from the kind of coloured plastic cup that my family only used for picnics. Everything in Del's kitchen was different from mine. The floor was covered in brown linoleum, worn threadbare around the door and the stove. The air smelt of chip fat and cigarettes. The bread was white and sliced. There were crockery cats and dogs sitting behind the glass of a plywood cabinet, the type they advertised on the back of tabloid magazines and which my dad, to my mum's infinite chagrin, sold in his shop. The bottle of salad dressing on the table looked like mayonnaise, not vinegar. Our dinner was beans on toast and fish fingers.

Del's dad ate his in the living room in front of the television and no one seemed to mind. Her mum ate hers at the counter, stopping to ask us questions (which Del refused to answer with anything more than gruff, monosyllabic grunts) or shout something through the door at her husband (his answers were exactly the same). I didn't know how I was supposed to behave, but I was only embarrassed when I thought of Del in my house.

My mum made things like spaghetti – not tinned or hooped – and stir-fries and chicken salad with different kinds of lettuce. And the three of us had to go into the dining room to eat it. We had to set the table, put coasters down, wait until everyone was sitting before starting. We had to have conversations. Watching television while eating would have been like walking down the street drunk and naked. You could tell my dad still wasn't quite used to all this – he'd joke with me while my mum was in the kitchen, make a pantomime of the formality, adjust an imaginary bow-tie, give me little conspiratorial winks like indulging her in this was our game. But he was proud of it too, I think, as though he'd managed to smuggle some exotic flower into his house and couldn't believe he'd actually done it – and that it'd survived. An orchid plucked miraculously out of its precious soil. A rose swaying atop a desert dune. His own father had worked making seaplanes at the local factory and the most outlandish thing he'd ever brought back was a Spanish hat from a holiday, that lay crumpled and half-devoured in the attic, eaten away by indigenous moths. And as I sat in Del's kitchen, listening to the canned applause on the television and the back and forth of the question-and-grunting session, enjoying being able to squeeze as much red sauce as I wanted on to my fish fingers, I tried to imagine Del and the others in my house and it filled me with shame. I pictured my mum asking them about school and things and then listening to their answers as though she'd just walked into a zoo and discovered the animals could speak. Then I pictured them staring at their plates as though they'd just been served monkey's brains and eyeballs.

After we'd finished eating Ricky and Neil came around. They sat down and Del's mother offered them tea and asked how Ricky's mother was and how Neil's father was. They both said fine (she hadn't asked me how mine were, even though she worked for them). And from the comfortable, accustomed way they were sitting I knew that their kitchens were exactly like this one.

Later, as we walked across the road towards the bus shelter, I tried – in rebellion against the slow creep of my envy – to see the village as my mum would. I sneered at the pebble-dash on the houses, arched a disapproving eyebrow at the couple in tracksuits who were arguing on their doorstep, looked up at the woebegone coal smoke coming from the chimneys and the dreary wet fields in the distance, and thought how dull and tacky and awful a place this was. It was a nondescript nowhere, in the back of a boring beyond. I pushed an imaginary plate of beans away in disgust. I identified Del's dad as an obvious wife-beater. I glanced at Del's glasses and whispered a silently condescending 'Poor thing'. But it didn't make me any happier and I suddenly resented it that Del never had to think about any of this, that when I'd come over she'd never even considered where she lived and what it was like.

It was early in the evening and a slight drizzle had begun to fall. Inside the bus shelter it smelt like damp ash and piss but I couldn't rouse myself to be properly offended or repulsed by this either. There was nothing to do, so we were grateful when Ricky shoved his hand into his jacket and pulled out a Lambert and Butler he'd stolen from his mum. It was slightly bent in the middle and some of the tobacco had fallen out of the end.

'Stump,' Del shouted immediately.

'Fli,' Neil blurted out a few seconds after.

I didn't know the village divisions of a cigarette, that a stump was from the writing down and a fli the last two puffs, or that they had to be called and claimed. Scavengers, I tried to think. Vultures, buzzards, gulls.

'Don't worry,' said Ricky, looking over at me like he was about to give me a pearl. 'I'll give you a few drags, yeh?'

I accepted them gratefully. I bolted them down.

Outside some younger children were kicking a flat football repetitively against the concrete wall of the shelter. It made a wet, slapping noise that seemed to syncopate and amplify our boredom. Yes, I congratulated myself, it was *so* boring here. Del couldn't stand still and paced around Ricky waiting for her stump. Neil was staring at his shoes, as though staring at the cigarette might be tempting fate. In the end the fli he got wasn't even one puff, and after he'd carefully scrunched the smouldering filter out on the ground we found ourselves peering down at it like it was some kind of broken toy. The ball thwacked against the wall, and as we waited for the next impact it came tumbling out on to the road and one of the children ran past the entrance to fetch it.

'Shit penalty,' he called back to some invisible failure behind the shelter.

'The Robinsons' is empty,' Ricky said, glancing towards me to make sure I'd heard. I didn't know what he was talking about. He'd wanted to run after the ball. I'd seen him twitch when it flopped by.

The Robinsons' windows were dark, inviting squares. In the ebbing evening light you could see the outlines of flower beds and apple trees in the garden. The village gardens we'd skirted to get here had been full of dead cars and sheepdogs and superfluous cats. Through the windows of the houses I'd seen the orange glow of electric fires and sad, immobile faces bathed in the ghost light of television screens.

'They're not in, Neil,' Del whispered.

We were crouched behind the wall, uncertain what exactly we were doing here.

'How do you know?'

'My mum says they only live here in the summer.'

Neil didn't look convinced.

'Fuck's sake, Neil,' Ricky spat. 'There's no one in there. Where's the lights, yeh? – they're not sitting around in the dark, are they?'

'I'll wait here.'

'Christ, Neil!'

'Leave it out, Ricky,' Del hissed. 'He can stay if he wants to.'

Then I realized we were going to break in. Thieves, I noted. Vandals.

Ricky and Del climbed over the wall. And, while Ricky stopped to help me over, Del crept over to the windows and began trying to prise them open. In the corner of the garden I could make out the surface of a fishpond partially covered in fallen leaves, the frame of a swing with a seat suspended from it on unseen chains, a boat covered in tarpaulin that looked like a giant pod or seed.

'These are locked,' said Del. It was getting darker by the second and her voice sounded thrown, like it was beside me, even though she wasn't.

'What about that one?' Ricky pointed to a small window on the corner, criss-crossed with thick black lines that divided its pane into diamonds.

'It's locked.'

'I can open it,' Ricky said, and I couldn't be sure if he was telling me this or Del. 'I can open it.'

He took out a penknife and slid it beneath one of the black strips, levering it carefully up, a few millimetres at a time. We hardly breathed as we watched him. I looked behind me towards the narrow track that led back to the road and the village. The shadows had swallowed most of it and the two village street lamps – one at the top of the hill, the other at the bottom – appeared stranded and distant, feeble lighthouses in a foggy sea. Neil sniffled somewhere in the gloom and it sounded ludicrously loud.

'See?' Ricky said, prising one of the diamonds out of the strips that surrounded it. 'Told you.'

Even though I couldn't quite make out his face I knew his eyes were little moles, grubbing through tunnels of dark towards the light of my approval. Del's face had faded into the glimmer of her lenses; a round, lidless owl's stare glistening in the dusk. Ricky's arm disappeared into the gap where the diamond had been and a few seconds later the window swung open.

Inside there was a silent kitchen. It reminded me of a book my dad had read to me when I was small child, about a baby who falls sleepily into a world of secret, midnight bakers. I vaguely recalled an image of them rolling the baby up in dough, and a moon made out of pastry. But this was the kitchen on the page before the bakers had arrived – the scary lull in the story when the child finds itself abandoned in an empty, adultless night.

Del began heaving herself over the sill before we'd had a chance to decide anything. It was what always happened – she always led the way – but I knew that this time Ricky had wanted to go in first and was sulkily hanging back. The window was directly over a sink and Del was trying to grab hold of the taps to drag herself through, but the narrowness of the window was holding her. Her stomach had begun to catch and bunch against its edges; it was folded against the wood of the bottom ledge. You see, my mum remarked in my head, you see what happens when you eat beans and fish fingers.

'Give us a hand here, Ricky,' she rasped. He came up dutifully behind her and pushed her through into the sink.

Then he turned to me. 'You coming in?' he asked.

I got through easily. I didn't even touch the sides.

Ricky was holding a sherry bottle up to the dark, trying to check how full it was, when the light began to creep across the kitchen wall. Faces appeared. A young woman gave us a slightly exhausted smile, while behind her two children holding butterfly nets glanced reluctantly in our direction. In the background I thought I could see sand and water, the iron stanchions of a pier, but before I had a chance to be sure the light had moved on to Del's face. She was taking a package of chocolate biscuits out of a cupboard.

Neil's voice came faltering through the window.

'Th ... there's a c ... car ...'

'Fuck,' said Ricky, the sherry bottle still in his hand.

The light glided over a chair and a table. It slid across a toaster and a spice rack, its progress so effortless and serene that it took me a few seconds to notice the lumpy heaviness that had filled my stomach.

'Where is it?' Del asked. Her voice was steady. She was calmly stuffing a handful of biscuits into her pocket.

Neil couldn't speak.

Through the window we watched as the headlights came up the track. Their beams were like white fingers, which, bored of caressing the house, had begun feeling their way into the shrubby undergrowth beyond the garden wall. The sound of tyres crunching over gravel filled up the darkness they'd left behind.

Ricky threw the sherry bottle out of the window and it thudded on to the grass.

'Let's get a move on,' he croaked. He didn't want me to hear how scared he was, but Ricky hated getting caught and for a moment he must have forgotten I was there. But in the few seconds it took him to scramble over the sink and out into the garden he'd had time to remember. His hand came reaching back through the window. Del and I both looked at it. And then, almost imperceptibly, she stepped beside me, put her hand on my back, and pushed me towards it. And the instant my feet touched the ground outside I realized I hated her for doing it. For all of it. For assuming I needed looking after, for the thought of her in my house, for not thinking about her house, for being able to eat baked beans and fish fingers for dinner, for knowing what a stump and a fli was, for having the same kitchen as Neil and Ricky, for trying to protect me from one that was unfamiliar, for not being afraid or ashamed or embarrassed of anything. And five months later I'd be thinking how I loved her for exactly the same things. Only by then it would already be too late. And I didn't know it yet, and I wouldn't know it for a long time, but it was going to become too late in the next few minutes.

Del was stuck in the window. As the car came closer she tried to haul herself through and her efforts became desperate and frantic. She twisted and turned and grunted. Her arms flailed around, making wild, breaststroke motions in the air. Biscuit crumbs came tumbling out of her pockets. Her glasses had fallen into the grass. She wasn't looking so comfortable in *this* house.

Ricky ran over and tried to drag her out. Neil was standing at the corner of the house, the upper part of his body swaying, as though it wanted to go to the window to help but the bottom part of his body wouldn't let it. I stayed back too. The lumps of fear and hatred in my stomach had got all mixed up – I wanted to get out of here but I also wanted Del to get caught. I pictured her humiliation. I tut-tutted with the driver of the car.

The sound of the tyres on the gravel was becoming deafening.

'Will someone please give us a frigging hand here?' Ricky hissed.

Up ahead walls and hedges flashed into view. A tree appeared and then abruptly dissolved. Startled animal eyes flickered and flared and vanished in the fields like showers of meteors. Neil and I didn't move. Neil couldn't. And then there were two red lights on the track and they were in front us.

The car had passed by without stopping.

As the sound of the tyres receded it was replaced by Del's breathing – low, shallow, staccato gasps that might have expressed relief or exhaustion or both. Her body had slackened and bulged pathetically over the window frame. Her arms had given up and hung limply against the wall . . . her hands waiting on its stones for mine.

'Cheers for the help, you two,' said Ricky.

Del said nothing. She asked for nothing.

And then I laughed.

'What's so fucking funny?' Ricky asked.

But I didn't answer. I just laughed. And I carried on laughing until Ricky didn't know what to do and so he started laughing with me. Neil didn't make a noise. He walked silently up to Del and tried to pull her out while Ricky and I laughed at her.

Her breathing had become slow and quiet. The darkness hid her expression. But if I'd been able to see her face, if I'd been able to see her naked eyes, then I might have known. I might have known right then and there that she'd leave me.

Neil

Past the estate, past the football field, past Spar, past the post office, past the chapel, past the bus shelter: Ricky's got the right idea – it's best to keep moving. There's pitfalls and detours and delays all around us here. Howsyourmothers and howsyourfathers and howareyous. They may look like they're floating but they've all got tongues. Flip the globe over and the snow will start falling. Let them speak and the words will come down in a flurry. They'll settle in front of us in drifts and banks. They'll suck our legs in and freeze our feet.

Ricky's better at it than me. His greetings are snow-shoes.

'A-right, Gruff.' A thumb in the air. A nod. A few quickened paces so as not to break through the surface. Tread adroitly, distribute and diffuse the weight.

'A-right, Jack.'

'A-right, Mrs Evans.'

And it's simple enough for Steph and me to follow in his safely compacted footprints: Steph's a stranger here and nobody expects me to speak, not even now.

We've almost made it through the village and it's been so much easier than I thought it would be. I've got past Del's house and discovered that the one place she isn't is at home. I've got past my father's house and I know I could speak if I wanted to.

I used to think that I'd lost all my words in that house. It seemed like the best explanation at the time, as good as any other at least. After my mum was gone my father and I would sit together while the silence spread around us and filled up all the rooms, one after the other. It was like she'd taken our voices with her, or tidied them away before she left us and put them someplace we couldn't find; as though, if only we'd searched properly, we might have found them – syllables hidden in the backs of drawers, sentences locked in cupboards, vowels caught in cobwebs in the attic. But neither of us looked. I don't think my father had the energy. His eyes were so tired back then. Sometimes they'd get so tired he'd hide them from me, like my mum had hidden the words.

I'm past both of the houses and I've nearly made it on to the bridge before I make the mistake of looking back. At first glance all I see is two boys loitering inside the bus shelter, smoking and playing with their phones, but after a second I notice that beyond the shelter's far wall a figure is moving. It's shuffling from foot to foot, impatiently, as if it's waiting for the boys to hurry up. But neither of them looks up from their phones. And then she turns round and stares right at me.

Her lips are mouthing silent, familiar words; telling me, asking me. And I want to say no, this time I want to say no.

'Come on, Neil, let's get the boat. From the Robinsons' yard.'

How can I hear this? Why can't I stop hearing this? I remember Doctor Roger telling Billy Bins, after he said he'd seen an old woman sitting on his toilet holding her decapitated head in her hands, that ghosts were just memories in the wrong time. But how can they speak? How can they walk towards me – opening a mouth in which I can see tiny crabs scuttling across teeth – and say, 'Come on, Neil, it's nothing. It'll be easy.'

'Let's leave it, Del,' I say. But I don't know who is speaking this. Is this me? Or a memory of me in the wrong time?

'Let's leave it, Del. Let's do something else. Let's wait for Ricky to get back from town.'

But already she's turned on her heels and started walking down the road, saying, 'It's all right, Neil, you don't have to if you don't want to,' knowing that I can't say no to her, knowing that I'll be following. And already we're huddled in the Robinsons' yard, waiting for the evening to thicken and hide us, watching as the bats that skim over the tops of the trees disappear into the gloaming, black stars vanishing into black holes. Your back's turned to me, Del, as you scan the track and check the windows (like you did before, all those months ago, with Ricky and Steph, before things were different, before they started changing) and out of your sight I stare at the rolls and undulations of your back, its rippling solidity, wanting to press my cheek against it – did you know that, did you ever know that? – wanting to tell you that you're the only one who can stop me feeling afraid (or is that unspoken sentence in the wrong time too, in this one not that one?). But already we're pulling the boat across the garden and on to the track, and the sound of the trailer wheels crunching over the gravel has filled the short space between us, the single sound in this evening which is so very still, as the days after will be so still, one after the other, until in the village they will all say they can barely remember an early spring as breathless and serene as this. Passing the school and cresting the hill, we will come upon a moon rising over the sea below us, silvering a line across the straits, a bridge of light that we will head towards. And the mountains will be darker than the night, and the mainland windows will begin to twinkle beneath them, and the sweat on your face will catch the moonbeams and glisten. Stopping to rest, you'll sit on the cold metal of the trailer, your breath heavy and exhilarated, just as mine is short and nervous, assuring me that nobody will see us and we haven't got far to go, only down to the beach where there's a place they'll never find. You tell me this like you know everything, Del, like the world will never hurt you, like nothing will. Not sticks or stones or words or anything else. And I believe you. You've dragged me so many places I didn't want to be but you've always dragged me out of them too.

Somewhere close by an animal coughs and my stomach flips and lands upside down and broken like an omelette. A beam from a lamper's torch strobes a field in the distance, trying to catch rabbits' eyes. The boat keeps getting heavier.

We're almost there, you say.

We come to where the road forks and follow it along the shoreline. The moon has made a landscape out of silhouettes, shapes cut out of dark – Carnedd Dafydd, Carnedd Llewelyn, the Orme, the dovecote domed like a minaret, a church on a hill with nothing left standing but its steeple, topped with a black cross. Out of sight, beneath the yew boughs, the waters of St Seiriol's Well are slumbering on a pillow of cold coins. The line of moonlight seems to follow us, sliding along the straits, keeping pace with our every step as though it were trying to catch our eyes.

The bell of the lighthouse chimes, once, twice, three times. Behind it Seiriol's Island is only an outline, unlit by a light that no longer shines.

We pull the boat into the lee of the rocks and then you pull me down over the white stones of the beach towards the wrackline, to gather sticks and branches thrown up by winter storms. And you must have known then, Del – by the way my body tensed, by the way I hung back, stiff and reluctant, so that you had to take my hand and lead me – you must have known that I could hear the sea lipping and sucking at the stones below us. With my hands full and the twigs pressing into my face, I could feel it creeping up behind me, stealthy and ravenous and octopus-armed. Between their tentacles there are snapping beaks.

Beneath the sticks and branches, wrapped in its tarpaulin, the boat is almost invisible. It looks like a giant seed, a triffid's pod. Nobody's going to find it, you say. And your hands rest briefly on your hips, satisfied with what they've done. It's well hidden, Del. So why can't we leave it now, please? Let's leave it hidden for ever and walk back together. Into the right time. The time we should both be in.

But already that seed has begun to open.

Steph

In the bus shelter the boys' thumbs tap out messages on their phones.

'Get a move on,' the girl shouts. Her face is thin and pointed, slightly desperate, possibly cruel. The hoops of her earrings almost touch the bottom of her neck.

The boys ignore her.

'Fuck's sake, we've been waiting ages now.' Her exasperation seems to pinch her skin even more tightly against her cheekbones, the same way her hair is drawn ruthlessly back from her forehead and across her skull.

'Are we going to town or what?'

One of the boys lifts his head up and eyes me with a bored, desultory lasciviousness. He can only be fifteen, at most. He answers her without looking.

'In a bit, yeh. There's no frigging hurry, is there?'

I have a brief premonition of this conversation repeated endlessly, bouncing back and forth through the increasingly frustrated years. I think she does too, because she turns angrily towards us and fixes us with a defensive and defiant glare.

'What *you* looking at? Perv!'

It's only then I notice that Neil *is* looking at her. I mean, he's really staring at her. He's stopped in the middle of the road and even when she shouts at him he doesn't turn his head away, he just keeps on staring.

'You gawping at me?'

The boys, who were nearly oblivious to the girl's words when they were directed at them, quickly shift their attention when they realize they're being aimed at someone else.

'What's your problem, pal?'

'You some kind of nutter or what?'

And I know they're just kids but there's something about Neil today, about the way his anorak billows out from his thin frame and his trousers are crumpled against his skinny legs, that makes him seem more like a kid than them. One of the boys stands up and spits in Neil's direction; the girl drifts proudly towards him, seeming happier now that they have a shared interest.

'Fucking freak,' she hisses.

Neil's eyes plead with her. His lips open and close but no sound comes out. Her eyes are sneering black holes.

Ricky's stopped ahead of us and I'm waiting for him to come back and help me. But he doesn't. And for an instant I'm tempted to walk away from all this, to turn on my heels and just walk away. It's stupid me being here anyway. It can't change anything. Suddenly this island and everyone on it seems as glazed and distant and unreal as the pictures in Mr Griffiths's books did, nothing more than a bad, mainland dream that I can snap my fingers and leave. But I don't.

'All right, Neil,' I say. 'It's all right.'

As I try to pull him forward my hand falls through the fabric of his anorak and lands on his ribs. They feel brittle, breakable. 'What's wrong?' I ask. And without thinking about it I'm whispering, as though he's so fragile my voice might snap him.

'What's with him?' the boy snarls, taking a few steps forward and pushing out his chest.

'Nothing,' I say, putting my shoulders back and looking straight at him. 'Leave him alone.'

'Wanker!' says the girl.

'Fucking weirdo!' says the boy as he sits back down in the bus shelter and returns to his phone.

'Fuck's sake, can we go now or what?' I hear her say as we walk on.

Up ahead Ricky's watching an old man walking down towards the bridge. He stops on the other side as if he's waiting to let us past. There's a faint snowdrift of chalk dust on the lapels of his heavy tweed jacket and he's narrowing his eyes to look at us, like he might know who we are. Or if he doesn't then he should.

Ricky

If it's not the last person in the world I want to see! I mean, I'm being dead honest here: if the Apocalypse had just fried the whole planet, if Steph and the Four Horsemen had just torched the entire frigging caboodle, and I was walking down this road through the ashes thinking what have they done, here I am alone for ever – like at the end of *Planet of the Apes* – and I saw him coming the other way, I'd run and get a box of matches and finish myself off. Or him, I suppose. There'd be no loneliness on earth that'd make me anything but gutted to set eyes on him. And if he saw me then I bet he'd be thinking, that Ricky, what's he doing here, he doesn't really come from the same scorched wasteland as me, does he? He's from a slightly different scorched wasteland. They burn a bit differently there. Mr Fucking Jones.

There's a double-take second when I spot him, a cartoony eyes-on-stalks kind of second. And it isn't like the fact I've seen him's this massive shock or anything. I mean, he lives in the village and it's not like I haven't bumped into every other living member of it already – honestly, it's been like the dodgems getting down the hill and on to the bridge, bump, bump, bump, don't get caught and pressed up against the side, don't stall and find yourself being moidered about that time you played the xylophone like an angel in chapel at the harvest festival and did you keep up the music – no I didn't, I was shit at music, that's why they made me play a moron instrument like the xylophone – and I wouldn't have been surprised if they'd started wheeling out the dead to boot. Here's Mrs Pritchard, she used to serve you chips in the canteen, had a bit of a stroke a few years back but we've dug her up out of the yard to say hello. My my, you've grown, haven't you, Ricky bach? Always one for second helpings, weren't you?

He's creaking down the grey asphalt road, stiff as the Tin Man. He's doddering, that's the word. He's old. And it surprises me 'cause I don't remember him as that old, but he must have been quite old even back then, to be this old now. He's shrunk too, like they've put him in for a wash on the wrong cycle and he's come out all crumpled and two sizes less. People get smaller. That's always kind of surprised me. My nain used to tell me she was five foot six in her slippers and her prime, but I couldn't get the head I was above her around the idea she could've been anything over the five foot two she was when she told me this. 'Oh no, I was this tall once,' she'd say, holding her hand above her head and looking up at it like it was the top of a beautiful mountain she'd just fallen off. I guess once you've toppled over the hill you've got to start walking on down the other side of it. But nobody actually tells you this is going to happen. In school there's only one way you're heading, apparently: forwards and up, Flash Gordon style. It's like them apes-to-men pictures they used to show us in biology, the ones where the chimp turns into the bigger, taller chimp, and then takes his knuckles off the floor and becomes this slouching caveman. And then a couple of figures on he's had a shave and a haircut, grown ten inches, and looks as if the next step's going to be right into a nice suit and a tie, as if evolution were a school teacher or an army sergeant hidden off the page somewhere, shouting you there, stand up straight, put them shoulders back, walk tall. But they never let us see the next step, did they?

Never let us see him walking small again. Never got to the moment when Sergeant Evolution has just got knackered, slumped on to an armchair in front of the telly, and started wheezing, do what the fuck you want, head anywhere you like, backwards is great – I don't know where we're going anyway. Apesville's as good a place as any.

But maybe there's a reason to it, this shrinking and crinkling? Maybe it's something to do with making you look like you need looking after, like you're a kid again. Near the end, when my nain was pretty much down to the size of a lemur, I'd get this impulse to blurt things out like 'There, there, mind how you go', and 'Whoa, slow down there partner'. I'd almost feel like giving her a pat on the head sometimes, though I would have got one hell of a whack with her walking stick if I'd tried. And so I reckon it's just as well that Mr Jones has done a bit of dwindling 'cause the first thought I had when I saw him was to go up and knock him right back into the last decade.

My fist was clenched and ready to go, I'm telling you. I wanted to feel it thudding into his face, I really fucking did. And then he's become this doddering old fella and I know I can't do it. There's this moment, right – when I know I know I can't – when my brain starts patting itself on the back, shaking its own hand, and saying good on you, mate, you've got a few years behind you now and you've learnt how to box a bit clever, to rise above this shit and let it be. Which is great – except that all the rest of me hasn't risen above anything: it's still flailing about in a cesspool, an octopus sunk in its own rotten ink. You see, my body's remembering again and I'm not liking it this time.

He's there at the end of the bridge. Mr Troll. Out of the corner of my eye I can see the great toadstool of smoke coming from the Candyman's and over the side of the bridge I can see a rat or something shuffling through the weeds on the river bank. Somehow it reminds me of this film I saw once when I was dead little, called *When the Wind Blows* – I'd always get it mixed up with *Wind in the Willows*, which was a bit weird – about this nice old couple trying to survive the aftermath of a nuclear war. Christ, it was depressing! They did everything they were told, put paper on the windows, made a shelter with a door to hide under, stayed indoors, listened for further instructions, and it made fuck all difference. Soon enough their hair's falling out, and their teeth as well, and the wife's saying things like 'I'm not feeling so good', and the husband's saying, 'Don't worry, we're going to be all right', believing that as long as he follows the instructions then it has to be all right, surely. It was a cartoon, but not for kids, I'm reckoning. Because for years after I thought this was definitely going to happen. Whenever I heard a bell or a siren I'd get all jerky and nervy and look out the window expecting to see a big cloud coming out of the horizon. And because I was a kid I didn't have any of those ha ha end-of-the-world thoughts, like who you'd shag if you knew it was going to be your last. No, instead I'd be thinking I had to get to my nain's so I could tell her stuff like that husband had, even though I knew it wouldn't be true. I'd get all distracted and frantic thinking this. And if I was in school when it happened I'd start not listening and getting clumsy and breaking crap, like rulers and pots of glue. Mr Jones thought I was doing it on purpose.

He's there at the end of the bridge.

He thought I was a chip off the wrong block. The harvest of a bad seed that had blown into the village – and then back out again – on a bad wind. I could tell by the way he looked at me, like he was always expecting my dad's feckless blood to start making me fuck things up, like it was inevitable, like I was out to kill Abel the first chance I got. He even disapproved of my dad's name, which my mum had kept for some reason: when he did the register he'd call out everyone else's full one, but I was always just Ricky. In private I was probably just the 'Ryan' boy.

So when I'd break stuff and get things wrong he'd get this knowing, frowning glint in his eye and call me up to the front of the class. My dad was blooming out of me. The weeds were taking root in Mr Jones's precious garden. And I'd have to stand there and open up my hand while he got his cane out from the corner. And as he lifted it he'd glance over at the rest of the class as if to say, this is what happens when you break a ruler, but it wasn't really saying that at all, that glance, what it was saying was this is what happens when a nice girl from the village lets a gyppo tinker pikey into her pants, this is what happens . . . and then down it'd come, thwack, on to the flesh of my hand, not because I'd broken a ruler from thinking the world was going to end but because my dad didn't have the right fucking genealogies, didn't speak the right fucking language, thwack, didn't sing and write poems and go to chapel and think these were the most important fucking things on this about-to-blow planet, thwack, because I was half of something and not the whole thing and he couldn't forgive me for it and so he was trying to smash it out of me, to beat out the corrupted part, to bleed it out over the welts on my skin as I stood there refusing to blub a single fucking tear thinking if I don't come from here you wanker then where the fuck else am I from!

There he is, at the end of the bridge, paused like he's waiting to charge us an admittance fee to go visit the rest of our island. Mr Toll. And I'd like to frigging pay him one too, five clenched fingers and a thumb's worth of one. The gears in the old Ryan generator are beginning to slip out of sync. Some of them are spinning around going, you're beyond this now, mate, none of that mattered, everything's different – and besides, today's about Del, not us, it's about Del who was the only one who looked at you when you were up there at the front of the class and let you know that she liked all of you and didn't give a flying fuck about anything you were or weren't, about anything you had or didn't have, the only one whose eyes didn't say, I'm glad I'm not you, I'm glad I'm not what you are. But there's others spinning the other way altogether and sending their electricity into my body, hot, prickly, pins and needles of it, making it remember when it doesn't want to, making it step back into where it doesn't want to be.

I've got to walk past. I've got to get over this bridge and then burn the bastard. That world has ended, Ricky. It's over.

Neil

My feet got stuck on the bridge. I could feel the cold water flowing beneath its stones, chilling the soles of my shoes. When Mr Jones said how are you, my mouth didn't work again.

I knew Ricky wanted to hit him. I've seen that face lots of times, in school, in town, at the end of evenings, when he'd look into people's eyes and seem to see something there – which I could never see – something that'd make him go suddenly quiet, as though he'd just walked into an empty room.

Mr Jones asked how we were again. But Ricky stared right past him and I couldn't speak. Steph's hand was pressed gently against my back, faintly caressing my xylophone ribs as if she were trying to comfort me.

'Get a fucking move on here, won't you, mate,' Ricky hissed at me beneath his breath.

The third time Mr Jones asked, I noticed how his face had changed. His skin was drooped and fell in folds from his jaw. It was paler than mine and hung against his neck like guttered wax. His eyes were glazed and glaucomous and reminded me of lamb's wool still wrapped in afterbirth. He began to frown suddenly, as though he'd only now realized something was wrong.

'You're late,' he said sternly.

It was his schoolroom voice, the one he used for morning prayers and admonitions. For a second I heard it as it was then, rising up to the roof of our little hall as some of us closed our eyes and bowed our heads, and others winked and nudged each other with their elbows . . . usually Ricky. *Ein Tad, yr hwn wyt yn y nefoedd. Sancteiddier dy enw.* Sometimes I was frightened of this voice. Sometimes I was frightened of Mr Jones.

'You're late,' he repeated. But out here in the open his words sounded out of place, echoes from a time that had already elapsed and passed; the clanging of the three o'clock bell, the clunk and click of a closing door.

I remembered how he had frightened me, but I also remembered how he'd tried to be kind to me when no one else was looking. He gave me a book once. It was wrapped in paper and he handed it to me as I was leaving for home. 'Give this to your father,' he said. But it wasn't for my father, it was for me. When my father unwrapped it he smiled and put it in my hands. It was an illustrated book, beautifully drawn: there was a picture of two dragons wrestling as a prince looked on; a princess dressed in white silk, brocaded with gold, who wept in a room as two birds stood in the window and sang; a giant, a pig, and a woman made of flowers.

Occasionally he'd invite me into his office – pretending he was going to give me a row – and then sit me down in a chair and talk to me, slowly and quietly, waiting patiently as I forced out my mangled answers. 'You're an intelligent boy, Neil,' he'd say. He'd teach me words I didn't know and help me to speak them. He'd tell me stories about my taid and my father and the island. And maybe then I could sense that his sternness beyond the office door was really only a kind of desperation, a stiff-lipped, back-pedalling effort to make us learn while we could, while he was there to teach us; to help us; to make us see that our small green corner was as important as anywhere else – before we left it, before we forgot it. As if I could do either.

Beneath their filmy coating the whites of his eyes flutter and pulse like jellyfish trapped in stagnant pools. I know he's not right. I know he's not well. Three months ago Gruff Glo was drinking in the George and he told Billy and me how they'd closed the school in the village.

'Jones has taken it badly,' he said.

'Like how?' Billy asked.

'Like badly,' says Gruff, spinning his finger in circles beside his head.

'Lost it, has he?'

'Wouldn't know what the plot was, let alone where it was. Wanders around telling people they're late for school and stuff like that.'

'No way!'

'Honestly, mate. I'm not joking or nothing. He gave Anne from Spar a hell of a row the other day. And he tried to hit Dafydd Post with a stick. I'm telling you, he did: "Put your hand out, boy," he says, "you just put your hand out right now." Poor Dafydd's standing there not knowing what the hell to do. Tells me afterwards there's a second or two when he almost does stick his hand out too, just from habit like, from memory. I'll tell you, Billy, we didn't see eye to eye a hundred per cent but you had to respect the old bugger, you really did. Forty years in that school! We'd all be a sight thicker there in the village without him.'

'So you say, Gruff, so you say . . . what they going to do with him then?'

'Don't know, Billy, honestly. Probably nothing for now. He can be a pain but he's harmless really – unless you're Dafydd's hand – so I hope they don't lock him up or any-thing . . . taught you as well, didn't he, Neil?'

Yes. Yes, he did. And I wish I could teach him something

in return now, something I learnt without him: that when you're not well it's best not to say anything, it's best to keep it quietly to yourself and not let anybody know.

'So what have you got to say for yourself, boy?' he asks Ricky.

I pull my feet up and force them to move. Steph's hand is still on my ribs and it's helping me even though I don't want it to. Ricky would have walked past if I'd not held him back. I know that look.

'Is this some kind of fucking joke?' he spits. I push the air out of my lungs and coax it over my tongue.

'H . . . h . . . he's not well, Ricky.'

'You're a prick,' he shouts. 'You're a fucking prick! That's what I've got to say, you old fucking prick.'

The boys from the bus shelter have stood up and begun to walk over. I look everywhere for Del but she's not there any more. She could've helped, I know she could've helped.

'Don't you speak to me like that,' he says.

The veins on Ricky's neck are throbbing. I know he wants to hit him, I know he's trying to stop himself. He trying so hard that he's begun crying.

'You fucking prick,' he gasps, his chest heaving now, not allowing him the breath to shout. And Mr Jones's eyes just keep swimming in their pools, as though Ricky's words were spindrift on a distant swell. And then Steph's hand has left my ribs and moved on to Ricky's shoulders. They're walking up the hill on the other side of the bridge and I follow them. 'The prick,' I hear Ricky sob into Steph's shoulder. 'The fucking prick.'

'You're late,' I hear Mr Jones say to the boys behind me.

Steph

The bridge is behind us. Beneath the olive sheen of Ricky's skin, which is still so smooth and soft after all these years, you can see the blood gathering, staining his complexion. In front of us the road snakes through a copse of trees, the leaf-buds clinging half-opened on their branches. Gravel tracks fork away on either side of it, their entrances marked by black plastic bins with green lettering on their sides. Verdant, they say – as if the spring needed prompting, reminding. They appear oddly familiar but who knows where they lead? Through the branches blink the whitewashed stones of cottage walls.

One of them leads to the Robinsons'. I know that. All I'm uncertain of is which one. But I never did pay attention, not once, not ever. And you don't, do you, not when there's someone else with you. You can walk through a place a hundred times with a person who knows it and it'll look like the daytime moon through a telescope: there's the seas and mountains and craters, all of them familiar, but seen as if through lunar dust darkly. It's the fallen sun that makes the moon truly visible. You only learn how to see things properly when you're alone.

It should've been so simple. All the houses here have names – everything has names, even the fields, even the woods – and most of them are engraved on slate at the end of their driveways or on their front gates. Around the village people use them for their own and so putting your hand on a gate or a doorknob is practically a handshake, an introduction. But I don't know which track leads from the Robinsons'. I didn't read the signs. If I had I might have realized that the direction we were headed in wasn't the one I thought it was. Because after the Robinsons' I began to imagine that Del and I were becoming best friends.

For a start, she began taking me places without the boys. The first time she turned up on her own, about a week after the Robinsons', I was watching Saturday telly. There were two belligerent knocks on the door – there would always be just two, and if I didn't answer quickly she'd be off down the street in a flash – and when I opened it she was standing there. I looked beyond the door frame to see if the others were loitering behind her like they usually did.

'Just me,' she said, almost smiling.

I forgot about leaving her in the window about as quickly as I forgot what I'd been watching. I was rather good at forgetting then.

'You coming?'

Del hardly ever bothered telling you where you were going. And if she did, it would be a simple announcement, never a suggestion. It was always take it or leave it with her, take it or leave it but I know you're going to take it. And I did.

Out on the street I felt that swift, sharp pang of resentment again, which I could never find a voice for, not even a protesting mumble, because before I'd had time to think about it I'd be stuck in Del's wake, dimly aware of my indignation as if it were already an afterthought, as though I were the victim of a hypnotist showman looking at the video of themselves squawking around a stage like a chicken. It was only about a hundred yards further down the street that it dawned on me that I'd actually wanted her to come inside my house. My mum was out shopping on the mainland (she didn't go to Spar like everybody else) and, without her in it, the house seemed more normal, more like other people's houses. I'd bought some records that I wanted to show to Del. I knew they were the right ones because my dad sold teen magazines in his shop and I read them carefully, preparing myself for acquiring that precious suffix which I was convinced would change everything. I knew they were the right ones but the girls I went to school with weren't impressed by them at all. They weren't interested in the expertise of a shopkeeper's daughter. Whenever my mum dropped me off at the school gates I wondered if she had ever noticed that her past meant nothing to them, that only my dad's present did; only my dad who was nearly bankrupting himself sending me somewhere to be subtly sneered at because of him. So I wanted to show Del what I knew, and I wanted her to be impressed by it. I wanted her to watch me put the needle on the record and smile at me, gratefully, thankfully. And instead I was out on the street, watching her back ripple in front of me, stuck in her groove.

That first time she took me to the old mansion, leading me up the steps and on to the roof where we stood – her leaning daringly on the railings – looking through the treetops at the fields sweeping towards the green and the straits; at the castle, with the town nestled apprehensively behind its walls; at the mountains, falling down to the mainland shore. And it seemed like there were three whole landscapes here, all different but crammed into the one vista, and that I'd never seen them at once like this. It was late in the autumn and there was smoke in the air, drifting up from unseen fires and distant chimneys, and the muffled explosions of fireworks which other children were letting off in the hidden nooks and crannies and corners of the island.

A few weeks later she took me to a rocky beach beyond

the village. It wasn't very far, but it was far enough for me never to have been there. To begin with, there was the usual blur of lanes and hedgerows and fields and cottages, and then we'd come upon the ruin of a church on a hill; it looked like a shipwreck, an abandoned Ark, except that instead of a mast and a figurehead it had a steeple with a cross on top. A few hundred yards past it there was another, intact, church, and beside it a strange, squat building with a conical roof of interlocking stones.

'What's that for?' I asked Del.

'Doves,' she replied, without slowing down, as though it was really quite obvious.

I didn't see any doves. In fact I'm not sure I knew what a dove looked like, although I may have had a vague image of them from a children's Bible, of squiggles that flew through rainbows.

There were signs in the car park beside the church but I didn't read them.

Del took a detour, away from the car park and into an enclosure of dark-green trees and slabs of rock. In the corner was a small stone shed with a pool of water in its floor. Del knelt down and splashed a few handfuls of it into her mouth. I cringed like my mum would've cringed. Del must have noticed.

'It's all right, it's a well. It's clean. Go on, you can drink it. It's lucky.'

There was a slight film of dust on its surface and on its bottom the coppery glimmer of coins. I thought of clammy hands and manure.

'I'm OK.'

'Go on, if you drink it you can make a wish and everything.'

I imagined sheep's tongues licking puddles and remembered watching a cow beside the castle lifting its tail and letting out a steaming, yellowy-green stream of piss.

'I'm not thirsty.'

'But it's lucky – it won't hurt you.'

Del wasn't budging, so I scooped a few drops past my lips and waited for her to turn around and head off. Then I quietly spat my mouthful of force-fed fortune on to the grass.

When we got back to the car park a coach had arrived and some pensioners were tottering off it. These came to the town in swarms during the spring and summer, and then in straggles in the autumn and winter. They had impressive, questing names, like Dragon Motors and The Western Express – somewhat at odds with their slumbering contents – but they rarely ventured further on to the island than the town. Del and I strode past the old people, who were gathering reverently in groups around the signs; ancient pilgrims wrapped in gaudy-coloured anoraks, come to sacred places picked at random from brochures.

After a few hundred yards we crested a slight hill and came to a beach of white stones, which had been swept into undulating peaks and troughs, petrified waves, as though the sea had heaved itself ashore and uncovered a Medusa's head. When I looked to my right I saw a lighthouse. And then an island. For a second I didn't quite believe they were there. Across the straits I could see the familiar outline of the mainland, familiar from the town at least; the shapes of the mountains told me that the town wasn't very far away and I tried to picture the view in this direction from the pier: there was the curve of the shore, a headland jutting out in the distance – but no lighthouse, no beach of white stones, and certainly no island. But then I thought again. Yes, the headland must be the island, it must've always been the island. And I stood there baffled that I'd never noticed this, that a few miles of shore and a particular perspective could have hidden an entire island from me. I still couldn't quite believe it. But then again, when I was with Del places always seemed to appear suddenly and unexpectedly. Or perhaps it wasn't just Del. Perhaps on islands places always appear like this, even other islands – like doors opened in the backs of wardrobes.

Del threw a stone into the sea and then looked at me with a mixture of amazement, possibly contempt, followed by suspicion. Her eyes narrowed behind her lenses. I'd asked her what it was called and she didn't believe I didn't know.

'Seiriol's Island,' she said. 'Or Puffin Island.'

'Who's Seiriol?'

'A saint.'

'What's a puffin?' Her eyes narrowed again.

'A bird, yeh? Like a penguin or something, that live in tunnels underground. You know.'

'And they live there.'

'Not now they don't. The rats ate them!'

The island wasn't that big. It was bunched up into a hill on one side, against a cliff, and then sloped down on the other, like a half-risen cupcake; there was a small stone tower on the hill for a blown-out candle. It was quite close to the shore but its cliff and ragged rocky edges made it look stark and inaccessible, and the narrow straits seemed to pinch the sea, making it seethe and squirm. The lighthouse stood about thirty feet off the shore.

Del clambered on to a black, uneven outcrop of rock that bounded the beach, and skipped from seaweedy ledge to seaweedy ledge, over pools and crevices and jagged clefts, without once slowing or faltering, without once even looking down. I slipped and stumbled along behind her, my heart beginning to beat too fast and my stomach lifting against my ribs. I could see barnacles and mussels everywhere, smiling at me with razorblade lips. Watching her, I couldn't understand how she could be so agile, how, despite her flabbiness, she could be so absolutely and unconsciously confident that her footsteps would come down safely, as though she were an acrobat and the rock beneath her were made out of marshmallows. She stopped and waited for me opposite the lighthouse. Up above some seagulls began circling and screaming.

'You can get there at low tide,' she said.

'To the island?'

'No,' she said emphatically and slightly irritably, as if my stupidity were not only astounding but rather wearing too. 'To the lighthouse.'

There were two birds standing on the base of the lighthouse. They were skinny and black, with long necks, and when they craned their heads to peer into the water they looked like question marks. I thought they might be puffins but I didn't want to ask Del. I was suddenly a bit sick of her knowing everything. I didn't really care what they were. And I would have left it at that if it hadn't been for a heavy emptiness that started to settle into the pit of my stomach and a tingling numbness that spread into the back of my head. It was exactly the same feeling I got when they ignored me in my school. The sea in front of me rippled and roiled. Somehow, instinctively, I knew what to ask.

'What's on the island then?'

'Nothing. Just rats.'

'So you been there then?'

I noticed her body tense, an infinitesimal tightening that pushed her lips together and forward; two shallow creases appeared above her nose, at the edges of her eyebrows. For an instant the vaguely satisfying image of her trying to swim out of the Robinsons' window returned to me – the flailing, hopeless arc of her arms through the air.

'We could if we wanted to.'

I wondered who that 'we' was and was suddenly convinced that it didn't include me. I carried on relentlessly. 'So you haven't?'

'It'd be easy if we wanted to.'

'Yeh, sure,' I said, throwing my chin up sceptically, smirkingly.

And then I set off back towards the beach. By the time Del had caught me up and overtaken me some of the pensioners had arrived and stood at its edge, not wanting to risk themselves on its loose stones. A cold, salty breeze had begun to blow off the sea and it made their eyes glisten and water and blink. I doubted if they could actually see anything, let alone Del and me as we walked past. Behind us I heard the lighthouse bell chiming.

Another time we went to an abandoned farm on the outskirts of the village, which Del told me had once belonged to Neil's grandparents. She said she remembered when they still lived on it, five or six years before, and that the grandfather had kept pigs in the back yard. We walked down the track and everything from before was forgotten. Del swung her stick at clumps of nettles and ran it playfully over the top of the barbed-wire fence that sagged along beside us. The fields were full of thistles.

We came to a barn on the edge of the farmyard. It was circled with a strand of plastic tape, which some builders must have put up, that made it look a bit like a crime scene, a flimsy effort to quarantine it from the tattered clutter of the surrounding yard and the other outbuildings; scraps of black silage bags flapped about on the ground like the wings of crushed bats; strips of corrugated iron clung precariously to rotting timbers; the mysterious bones of old machinery poked out of the mud. On the far side was a cottage with bushes growing over its windows. The tape was no defence against Del, who instantly slipped under it and went to look through the half-boarded doorway. She was always drawn to places which appeared prohibited or forbidden, places you probably weren't supposed to go. I think she believed there was nowhere you shouldn't be allowed to go.

'It's empty,' she called back to me.

But it wasn't empty. It was full of hay bales, stacked almost to the roof.

Up above Del's face flits back and forth over the parapet of the bales, smiling with a child's impishness as she throws clumps of hay down at me. The long-dormant dust leaps out into the air, releasing an acrid, musty smell, thick with old animal sweat and dead summers, and the hay rains on to my hair.

'Stop it,' I shout, 'stop it . . .' But my words trail into giggles as I climb after her.

At the top I try to grab her foot and she squirms away into a tunnel between the bales. It feels warm up here, as if there were shards of remnant sunshine in the stalks, and it makes me giddy and reckless. I follow her into the tunnel and some-thing sharp grazes my hand and sticks to it – a rose sprig, holding to my palm by its thorns – and as I pick it off the desiccated petals of the flower break away and flutter back on to the floor of the tunnel. My hand could be bleeding but it doesn't hurt.

The tunnel ends in a snug chamber, with the corrugations of the roof above and walls of hay all around. There's barely enough room for the both of us so I squeeze up beside Del and we lie there, staring up at a spider's web and catching our breath. Thin lines of damp light sneak under the eaves but they can't touch us here. Everything outside is far away. Del begins to fidget and turn, pressing the soft folds of her belly against my ribs, and I can feel her wriggly, feral warmth against my bones. She's speaking but I'm not quite hearing. I'm so comfortable here, I don't think I've ever felt this comfortable. There's no need to think. The dust swirls in slow circles and I can smell the chocolate on her breath, sweet and bitter and sugary. My replies come out prickly, as though I've swallowed hay, and there's a low, gorsey roughness in my voice. It's a scarecrow's whisper. And then I have swallowed hay, most of the handful of it that Del's just pressed on to my face. She's rolled over and trapped me between her knees. Even if I wanted to I probably couldn't escape – her legs are strong, unexpectedly muscular – but I don't want to. I don't want to leave here. Half-blinded and suffocated by the hay stalks, with Del's face laughing above me, with a lightness in my head that is like dizziness, I want to let go of everything. My closing eyelids seem to snap anchor chains and my head begins to float upwards of its own volition, like a balloon.

And then I can feel the streaks of light on my face, their dampness and coldness. Opening my eyes, I find that Del has gone and my mouth is poised, slightly open, waiting, over vacated air. The places on my body where she pinned me down are suddenly chilly and I'm alone in a dirty, musty shed, looking at the bottom of her heels as they squirm away through the tunnel.

'It's empty,' she'd said. And it was then.

If I try, I can picture her standing by that door again, her sweater bunched around her shapeless waist, her glasses slanted unevenly across her face, her features filled with that unlikely, pig-headed, brave, almost absurd conviction that anywhere that wouldn't let her enter wasn't worth entering. I can picture her there clearly. She's so much easier to catch hold of in memory. And yet why is it hard for me to complete that picture, to form an image in my mind of myself as I watched her? It's always me who's missing. And however many times I attempt to conjure that other Steph into the frame, what I end up finding is irrevocably blurred and disfigured, a Halloween mask melted in the ashes, its features contorted out of all recognition into grotesque shapes of want and anger and love and envy.

I couldn't even read the signs on my own face. I didn't even know what they were.

Neil

Steph was laughing at Del and I hated her for that. It was because she wanted Ricky for herself. I saw her laughing and I could feel myself hating her, as if my skull was suddenly shrinking and pinching my brain. That's what hating felt like then. She was wearing her mother's perfume and that's what it smelt like: a stinging, chemical smell that went right to the top of your nose and on to the back of your throat. My feet were trapped on the dark ground and she was making Ricky laugh too and I hated him for doing anything she wanted. Even in the night I could see the golden curls of her hair sprayed into place and I wanted to tear them out and make her stop. Del couldn't get out. And I thought that if she couldn't then I couldn't. When I helped her I saw the way she looked at Steph and I knew that she hated her too.

PART FIVE

The School

Ricky

I'm thinking about Llew again. Why did he put up with it?
Prancing about for every hick and joskin in the Principality.
Didn't he have a moment when he thought, hey, I'm a bear,
Prince of the Forest, so you puny humans can all just piss off?
Why didn't he lash out? They'd taken all his sharp bits off,
but he was still a bear and surely you can take the bear out
of the woods but you can't take the woods out of the bear.
Was he ever homesick? And where the fuck did he come from
anyway? I've been thinking about him all day; he just won't
stay put. Don't ask me why either. I've not thought about him
for ages, for years, and you'd reckon I'd have bigger bears to
fry right this minute; like how I was so glad to get back here
and now I wish I'd never got into my car in the first place; or
like how, after a frigging decade, Steph's decided it's OK to
touch me. And it's not quite the way I would've chosen . . .
but what the hell.

It's a mystery to me why he's decided to come loping back
now. Or maybe it's not such a huge mystery 'cause I used to
think about him loads when I was a kid. I'd be asking my
mum stuff about him all the time like where he was from and
what he looked like, and she'd brush me off with saying he
looked like any other bear and he was from Wales. But I knew
that was bollocks, the same as when she read me this crap
about Christmas and when there were wolves in Wales. And
after a bit I stopped asking her 'cause she'd started looking

at me a bit funny and tired and suspicious by then, as if there was something wrong with me being interested in a stupid bear that'd been dead for ages. She said that once too: 'He's dead, Ricky, he's not here, so why don't you just shut up about him?' And she was beginning to look at me like that more and more then, even if I wasn't pestering her about Llew.

That's when I started spending most of my time at my nain's. She never looked at me like that, and she was happy to talk about Llew at the drop of a hat. Christ, once you got her going there was no stopping her. She said he was from Russia. I loved that. I imagined lots of ice and snow, blokes wearing big furry hats, flags covered in in hammers and sickles, and what the fuck if the Ruskies were going to blow up the world – I liked them a whole bunch better knowing Llew was one of them. At least I'm pretty sure he was one of them. I've had these doubts today 'cause Russia was bigger then, wasn't it, and maybe he was really from one of them 'stan' places, a Kazak or an Uzbek or whatever the hell they're all called. Talk about the goalposts always changing. Llew's one thing yesterday and then some bloke in a furry hat meets another bloke in a furry hat, signs a piece of paper, and he's another thing. It would've driven me nuts back then but I'm all right about it now. It's more important that Llew was a bear, to be honest, and that he could dance to boot. I can see that now, at least I reckon I can.

That's what my nain always let on too. She was happy enough to give him a past and a half like, traipsing through revolutions, downing vodka with woodchoppers, chasing princesses, hanging out with the reds – the whole fandango, I'm telling you – but once my great-grandfather got his hands on him . . . well, he was just old Llew then, a part of the family and their adventures. And what she meant was that all that stuff was great, yeh, a real yarn, something to be proud of, but in the end it didn't matter that much, not enough to have your head spinning like a top with it the whole day through, moving fast and not getting anywhere. She'd say that the thing about her whole family – and she always meant the Fair one, not the blood one, the entire crowd – was that they didn't have to be in a particular place to know who they were. In fact it was the opposite: it was because they weren't that they knew they were.

But what about now though, I'd think. What about now when you're stuck in this caravan that's not shifted for so long the rubber on the wheels has rotted? And fuck, she was a smart one, my nain, 'cause I only needed to think this, not even say a word, for her to know and answer me: 'It's in here,' she'd say, pointing her finger to her head as though she still got around just dandy up there.

And I knew she was angry with my dad for leaving her behind here – and me as well, I suppose – but she was proud of him too in a way, for doing the same thing. Like one of those Indians who got left behind by their tribe 'cause they were too old to keep up; not liking it, but appreciating that at least it was honouring the traditions. And bless her, she took it well. A whole fucking distance better than my mum. It must've been harder for her too, I reckon, 'cause when she'd come here with my dad they'd never planned to stay, she knew it wasn't part of any deal.

They were down to the butt end of that old life then, I guess, the last fli of it, with nothing much left but a bit of its memory and momentum; a boat coasting along after its engine's gone kaput. She'd grown up in its final gasps and my dad must've been born in its death-rattle. It was sad, she said, but nobody wanted dancing bears any more, or tarot readings, or bearded ladies, or midgets, or fat men, or bare-knuckle boxers – though the dodgy farming gear off carts carried on a tad longer. It was sad, she said, remembering how it began to die away and fall apart, the life, the family – unbearably sad. And how afterwards, without it, they became freaks. And the funny thing was they became freaks because they weren't allowed to be freaks, because they weren't allowed to put themselves on billboards and dress up and show themselves off to the punters in the tents. They had to go down the dole instead, and have some kid on the street shout Mum, Mum, that woman's got a beard, or some shop girl whispering, look at the size of that fat bastard, or some fuckwit in the pub moaning about pikeys to his mates. Suddenly they weren't special any more, they were just different. And then I was glad that Llew'd carked it before all that happened, that he'd been allowed to be a bear till the end and not have to spend his last days all fucked up 'cause he wasn't a dog or a cat or a cow or a sheep or any of the animals that lived round here.

Bloody hell, that hand on my shoulder! A decade late, Steph, a decade and some. I wish I could tell you that. And I wish I didn't care, that I didn't even notice it.

'There's loads of time,' I said that day. And I knew there wasn't.

But I was the stupid one. Letting you make me jump through any fucking hoop you wanted, dancing for you when you weren't my family, not even a punter, not even interested. And me ready to do jigs on cliff tops for you, to moonwalk right into frigging space.

But what planet was I on, honestly! Because I started out reckoning it was you who was doing the running.

'Why don't you come over?' you say.

It's dark and my heart's pounding anyway. We almost had it there in the Robinsons'. It's a miracle that car didn't stop. Boom boom boom it's going.

Neil and Del are a few yards ahead. They're in a mood and I know it but it doesn't make me catch up and smooth things. I don't think you even notice.

'Now?'

'Not now, later. Tomorrow.'

'We can come after school, yeh?'

'You can.'

And it takes a second but then it's sinking in that that you is me, just me on my lonesome. And the others are suddenly a hundred miles in front; or I'm a hundred behind, off in another village altogether, where the streetlights look different – brighter, more twinkling – and the houses have all been renovated into palaces and dashed with stardust, not pebbles.

Boom boom boom it's going. And if you cut me open you'd find my chest full of mushroom clouds and great balls of fire tumbling through my veins.

They're still going when I get to your door. They've tumbled me the whole way there. And you're waving down from the window like I have just walked over the moon and you're that over it to see me. But it's not Ricky the spaceman who's in action today, it's Ricky the fucking space cadet, not hearing a word from ground control to tell him you're only waving 'cause you don't want me to knock on that door, you don't want your mum to open it and find me there.

'Oh,' she says. 'You must be one of Stephanie's friends.' And for friends I'm hearing something else, like it's a word you might have to handle with rubber gloves.

'Ricky,' I say.

'Ricky . . . yes.' She's looking at me but she's not looking at me either, like she's half thinking about going off to get some disinfectant to put on her eyeballs. She's dressed up as if she's off to some cocktail party or something, with her make-up done all sharp and perfect, Egyptian style. Her eyes are in mascara boxes, gift-wrapped and not properly unpacked. But what the fuck, it's not as if I'm not used to people looking at me like this – even my mum's looking at me strange these days – and the sound of Steph on the stairs behind puts it right out of my head.

She doesn't even get down to the last step.

'Come on, up here, Ricky.' She's that keen, I'm thinking. Dead eager. She's not just doing the running, she's doing the hundred-metre hurdles. And there's only the one left.

'Stephanie, aren't you going to introduce me to your *friend*?'

'Mum, Ricky. Ricky, Mum. Come on, Ricky.'

'And so where do you live then, Ricky?'

This last one's turning into a real frigging pyramid. And Cleopatra here's trying her best to find more of her nose to look down at me over.

'The village, yeh.'

'Ah . . . yes. And so how do you know Stephanie then, Ricky?'

'*Mum.*'

'I'm talking to Ricky, Stephanie.'

It's stinking of polish in this corridor. It doesn't smell of anything else at all. There's a fur coat hanging up on a hook – who the hell has a fur coat round here! No, you're not talking to me, you're talking at me. For a second I'm thinking that's bear's fur. Pull yourself together, Ricky. Best behaviour. Just one more little jig to go. Those stairs are the promised land, remember.

'I'm mates with Del.'

'Oh, that's nice.'

'*Mum.*'

Yes, isn't it? Only I'm having a bit of a flashback of me sneaking off after school today; to me trying to skulk out the gates and Del and Neil catching me up and saying they're off to the shelter or something and then waiting around for me to go with them. And it's not even like anyone's got to say or ask anything 'cause of course I'll be going with them, I've

been going with them for so many years it's not as if I'm
going to have to check my frigging diary and clear a few
hours. But I'm not going with them, am I? Nah, have to go
home, I say. Which is such a big load of bollocks it's got
to be as visible as a pair of giant air balloons. I never have to
go home, I've been spending as much time away from home
as humanly fucking possible – which suits me fine 'cause I'm
sick of my mum looking at me like that, and it suits my mum
fine 'cause I'm getting this feeling that looking at me's making
her sick – and they know it. All right, says Del. Neil says nothing. And as I scuttle down the lane I can tell it's not all right,
that they're pissed with me about last night anyway and now
I'm somehow making things worse. And for a few yards I'm
feeling kind of shit about this; I can feel my lie floating above
me for everyone to see, tugging at the back of my head like
it's attached to it with a cord. But then the explosions are
going off in my chest again and they've blown that cord to
smithereens; those balloons are off into the stratosphere, way
beyond the clouds, and I'm almost skipping into town. I'm
like Llew, off to the teddy bears' picnic.

'Well, it's been nice to meet you, Ricky.'

Well, hasn't it just? You can go off and wash your hands
now. For a second it's occurring to me that it's strange I've
never seen her before – on the street, in Steph's shop, anywhere. I mean, you'd reckon I'd clock her, someone in that
get-up in these parts, but in the same second I'm hoping I
won't be seeing her again, not anytime soon.

Upstairs those boats are rolling on the cotton swell. And
I'm thinking this last leg of the journey's going to be the
easiest and shortest, a jaunt, a few feet across the duvet. In
fact fuck it, I don't think I'm even going to have to finish this
trip – I've got it into my skull that *you*'re going to. I mean,
I'm no Casanova or nothing, I'm only a kid, but in my
experience once you get this far then that's it, game over,

mission complete, things'll just happen; like when Tracy invited me round hers and I barely shut the door before her tongue's stuck in my gob. I'm happy as Larry. I'm happy your whole house stinks of polish. And I'm happy that you're nothing to do with my village, that you're from another school – I'm even a tad happy that your mum's stuck-up and weird – 'cause sitting here it's as if I'm not either. This is like a holiday, and as long as I'm here with you all that other crap is miles behind. I'm way off over the rainbow and everything looks brighter – there's new colours, there's the light on your hair and it's golden, Steph, a crock of flaxen gold. Somewhere back over the horizon there's this grey, murky place, where Mr Jones and my mum live, but that doesn't matter. They can go fuck themselves. They can go fuck each other, I don't care.

And then what happens? Nothing happens. Nothing. You don't shift an inch towards me. The wind must've died in those boats' sails 'cause nothing's shifting. This bed's seeming like the Pacific: quiet, yeh, horribly, awkwardly quiet – but massive as well. I can see myself in the mirror, a right hopeless case, waiting and waiting as if I'm drawing straws with myself to see who goes overboard. And there's this photo of a bloke on the mirror, with a big wedge of gelled hair dangling over one side of his face, and the other half sneering at me. What's the problem, Ricky, cat got your tongue, can't make your move – you frigging loser? Look at me. Can't fight these birds off, Ricky, they love me, they'd rip their knickers off if I lifted one of my eyebrows or blinked one of my faggy made-up eyelashes. They lie in bed *dreaming* of me. And look at you, mate – you're on her bed, and she's dreaming all right, she's half a-fucking-sleep with boredom. Christ, I want to go punch his smug face in. But Steph catches me eyeing him and must get the wrong idea entirely, 'cause she only gets up and starts playing one of the tosser's records. It starts out with all this bleeping and jangling and I just know what the bloke's voice is going to sound like, squeezed smarmily right out of the top of his nose. Hey, Ricky, watch how it's done, pal.

'We're no strangers to love
You know the rules and so do I . . .'
Except you don't, do you? Ha ha. Of course if *I* was there . . . bleep, bleep, bleep, jangle, jangle, jangle . . .

'. . . never gonna let you down
Never gonna run around and desert you . . .
Never gonna say goodbye
Never gonna tell a lie and hurt you . . .'
You see, Ricky, it's all a matter of sounding like a real stand-up, make-you-breakfast-in-bed, do-anything-for-you kind of bloke. 'We know the game and we're gonna play it . . .' Except that I do and you don't, do you? So let me give you a tip: look at her, she's thinking you're gonna be impressed by my crap, so you better pretend to be. Don't, for fuck's sake, let on you're having your flashback again. There's no room for that shit in the game, Ricky.

So I'm sitting there making out I'm actually *glad* to be hearing this. And what I'm not realizing is that everything's turned around. You're not doing the running, you're not even doing the walking, not even the frigging crawling – it's me who's doing it. Day by day, inch by inch, getting nowhere slow. This is difficult. This is never going to stop being difficult. And I don't even know why you wanted me there, Steph, all those times when I should've been with them, who did want me. Trying and trying, ready to do whatever you wanted me to do. So why should I care? Why should I even feel your hand on my shoulder, which isn't helping, which isn't taking anything away, which isn't changing anything.

How did you hold back, Llew? Alone in the tent, with their drunk breath jeering you on and their strange, sweaty faces leering and laughing at you; maybe remembering those old forests and fields of clean snow and ice, or the caravan with my nain, a little girl then, feeding you cakes and brushing your fur. Did you ever wonder if you could just dance another way, right into the middle of them, swinging your paws and battering them all away? Would it have made a difference? Would you have sat down on the ground, relieved, with nobody but your Fair family around you, and thought, there, I've done it. Would it have made you feel happy, just for a second?

Neil

We carry on up the road, underneath an overhanging lattice of sycamore and ash boughs – whose leaves are always the last to arrive, to find their way out of their thick, black buds – and past the entrance to the Robinsons' drive. Look at the starlings in the trees. Up close their feathers are many-coloured. The sky returns and the road begins to rise up the incline of a hill. A stray gull is dancing in a field. Or at least it appears to be dancing. My taid told me they do this to make the worms think it's raining and come to the surface. I notice how its vile and hungry eyes are peering into the grass.

The school sits on the brow of the hill, looking down on to the folds and creases of the island's ancient face, where the houses cling like white flakes of lifeless skin. The school building has shrunk – as I suppose they all do when we leave them – and become another place, a heap of remembered pieces that no longer quite cohere, just as memories will not: an arch, a rusting bell, an iron gate painted a pastel, unnat-ural shade of green which, in rebellion against the season, is being shed in leafy scales; at the back a wall – not so high these days – enclosing a square of crumbling concrete, where surrounded by fields we spent our days trying to play, cramped together, flaying our elbows and knees on chips of loose stone and cement while just beyond the animals munched on soft clover; a small yard, with a row of plastic milk crates and Lilliputian bottles heaped in the corner, still there, still empty – Mrs Thatcher stole our milk, that's what my dad told me; two doors, incongruously tall and arched, with 'Boys' engraved in stone above the one, and 'Girls and Infants' above the other. The long-ago divisions. We were meant to enter in preparation for how we'd leave, to learn what was waiting for us when we finished.

Ricky and I stop and stare for a moment through the railings of the gate. It's so quiet. A churchly calm surrounds it, a cloisters hush, and it takes a second or two to notice what is unusual about this. There are no children. Through the windows of a classroom I glimpse a circle of chairs placed upside down on a round table, as they were always meant to be placed at the end of the day; but I know that the end of that day has passed, long ago and irrevocably and for ever.

I startle as the door begins to scrape open. It catches on some stray pieces of gravel and a head creeps fussily around it, pointed disapprovingly towards the obstinate stones. It's cowled in one of the plastic hoods that most of the older women from the village wear at least until May, not trusting the fickle blue skies of April (just as I don't). A leg follows the head, and I recognize this instantly: the bland brown of the stocking, the colour of a tailor's dummy's counterfeit flesh; the sturdy, frustrated bulge of the calf. Miss Roberts. Always Miss. As the rest of her squeezes through, the head rises and becomes her face. She remembers ours without having to think.

'Neil, Ricky . . . and how are you? Well now, what a surprise.'

The stones beneath the door continue to distract her. Her foot edges subtly sideways, giving them a gentle, coaxing nudge, the same way her hand used to ease me out into the yard at break-time when I didn't want to go.

'Yes . . . what a surprise . . .' she says, testing the swing of the door with one hand and adjusting her hood with the other. There are yellow flowers imprinted on it, and beneath them the greying undergrowth of her hair. Having composed herself, she turns directly towards us, cupping her hands together in front of her waist as though she's ready to begin our times-tables.

'And so how are you?'

From behind the railings Ricky and I both say all right in turn: Ricky first, me second, same as on the register.

'Good. That's good. So you're both well.'

We both nod. All right. All right. Repetition was how we were taught.

There's a pause and involuntarily I begin to sway from side to side, shifting my weight from one foot to the other, as if I needed to go. Ricky's pulling a strip of paint off the gate and rolling it like a cigarette in his fingers. Miss Roberts can sense our concentration slipping.

'I'm so glad to hear that. I wonder where all of you get to these days, I really do. Off abroad and everywhere, I'm sure. I can hardly keep track, I swear.'

I can see her looking at Steph as though she's a souvenir we've brought back.

She should ask us about our mothers and fathers next, which is village decorum – and then aunts and uncles and nains and taids and cousins, and then their friends and acquaintances and ad infinitum – but Ricky and I have missing branches in our family trees and Miss Roberts, as she has always done, reaches adroitly past their stumps.

'And now you're back for a visit. Come to see the old place again. Well, isn't it nice to see you.'

This should be our signal, the ringing of the bell. I'm about to say yes, we were just passing by and thought we'd take a look. They were good times, weren't they? Nothing's changed. Everything's changed. Time flies. It does, doesn't it? Isn't it amazing, the way it does that?. Best be off. Ta-ra now, Miss. Always Miss (not everything). But Ricky speaks for and before me (no, nothing has). Yes, he says, a stroll down memory lane. And hasn't it been good to see the place, still looking the same. It does, she says, and then pauses. But not for long, she tells us, in her solemn morning-service voice. They've closed the school, don't we know?, almost a year back now. No, says Ricky, theatrically aghast, they haven't. They have, she mournfully assures him. There weren't enough children in the village to keep it open. Such a shame. Ricky nods his head. And so what now? Flats, she says, they're going to turn it into retirement flats. And so the old people have arrived here too, I think. Those withered and wombless Pied Pipers have whistled us away.

Ricky has sympathy and sadness on his face, mixed with a mild and appropriate outrage. Isn't that just awful, he says, shaking his head from side to side. Isn't it, she says, shaking her head too. It is, he agrees. Just awful. But I can see something else in that face now, a thought that has already occurred, a calculation already made. How soon, he asks, before they begin? A couple of months! He repeats this several times, chorusing the imminent tragedy. Maybe . . . he says, waiting a few seconds to make sure this sounds like it's occurring to him as he speaks . . . maybe it'd be all right for her to let us to go inside and have a last look at the old place, before it's too late, before they begin. Would it? But of course it would, it would be no problem at all, a pleasure.

Ricky pushes open the gate and steps into the yard.

Inside the corridor she appears more like Miss Roberts than before. Her feet are grooved on to invisible yet familiar trackways, cleaving to the left, always the left, as we were taught to do ourselves from the moment we arrived, learning our first valuable lesson about living safely in the world: always keep to the left. She walks at a school pace, not recklessly fast, not dawdlingly slow, and her voice sounds like hymns and psalms.

'It sounds silly, I know, but I like to keep an eye on it, boys. While it's still here. Habit, I suppose.'

The corridor, which once seemed wide and echoing, is now a muffling cocoon of bricks and slate flagstones. Miss Roberts's speech fills it, swelling against the walls, rising up towards the ceiling, and then hanging thwarted in the stifled air, like so many sighs trapped in a tomb.

'And I worry too, boys, I do, about people breaking in. Honestly, it was only last week someone got into Mr Thomas's car in the village. And it was parked right outside Spar! They come down here now, you know, all the way from Liverpool and places like that, just to steal things.'

Ricky nods his head, the perfidy of the mainland apparently weighing heavily upon him. I catch Miss Roberts glancing at Steph.

There are only two classrooms in our school and she unlocks them both for us. One is hers, where we stayed until we were old enough to go to Mr Jones's. Girls and Infants. Women and Infants too.

I wonder how we ever fitted in here. The tables are so small. The stack of plastic trays where we stored our crayons and pictures and numbers and spelling seem hardly bigger than my hands. They're nameless. We used to write ours on strips of white tape, cut carefully with scissors, and stick them on to the trays so that the whole stack would appear to totter slightly on seams of shaky, crooked letters. The chairs are doll's-house furniture. When I look up, Miss Roberts has sidled behind her giant's desk and I think she wants us to sit in them, to pull them off the tables, place them gently down, and begin all over again. To open the register and go back. Neil Thomas. Yma. Here. Here at the beginning. And if I could, Miss, I would. I would shrink backwards in time with you.

I remember watching a storm approaching through these windows; the clouds bubbling out of the cauldron of the Devil's Kitchen and streaming over the Carneddau, over the peaks of Dafydd and Llewellyn – scalding the Princes – and then darkening the white horses that played on the surface of the straits. On it came, the thunder rumbling, the lightning flashing over the mainland towns, illuminating the pale, cowering houses of Llanfairfechan and Penmaen-mawr. We shifted nervously in our chairs, wishing our island could detach itself from its foundations and flee further into the sea. And Miss Roberts, who saw how frightened we were – even Ricky, even Del – began to count: one two three, she counted . . . *un dai tri* . . . telling us that this was how you measured the distance of a storm, by the seconds between the thunder's clap and the lightning's flash. We counted eight with her, then six, and the storm lumbered on to the island's shore and swallowed the town, its forked tongue darting across the tops of the monkey woods, then three and the village below us had gone, lost beneath a crackling tumult of cloud and rain and electricity. In the fields beside the school the cows huddled against the hedgerows, their heads turned mournfully and stoically earthward, like people staring into graves. We counted two as the world outside became almost invisible, the rain blearing the windows and the clouds mass-ing above us into a midday night. And then one. But by the time we'd reached it, and the storm stared down at us through the nought of its Cyclops' eye, we had all become still and calm in our chairs, as if we had come to rest beneath the chalked and impregnable lean-to of a long division. Somehow the numbers, and Miss Roberts's recital of them, had soothed us, had insinuated into our minds – if only for a few moments, if only for the duration of the recital – the idea that in all this chaos of elements there was an arithmetic, an orderly sequence, a set of calculations that, conjured by the Pythagorian music of her voice, would eventually end in a blue and settled sky. I would go back to that moment with you, Miss. If I could, I would sit down and rest with you in that still, calm centre.

But Ricky drags us into the other classroom, where the chairs and tables are bigger. Miss Roberts skirts around them more carefully, more severely, like Mr Jones is watching her and she has to pretend to be strict, like she's waiting for his approval to fall across her stout hips and touch her painted lips. And I realize that she must have been waiting for it the whole time we were here, that maybe she's never stopped waiting. The perfume, the make-up, the hair so carefully done, they were never for us, I realize. They were for him. And we were the wayward children they never had together. I can remember the feel of coarse brown nylon being pulled over my thighs, and the mothering whisper that was not my mother's: 'Oh, Neil bach, what are we going to do with you, what are we going to do?'

The chalk on the board is fresh. Everything else is covered in a coating of pale dust – the chairs, the tables, the trays, the posters on the walls, even the air, where motes of it hang static and stranded in frozen carousels, unmoved by the momentary shock of our breath. Insect tracks trail along the floor, tiny footprints that look petrified; the marks of dinosaur feet sunk and fossilized into the residue of ancient eruptions, the fall-out of dead volcanoes. And in this parched and powdery stagnation, so dry that it has sucked the moisture out of my mouth, that chalk is as fresh as pollen.

There are numbers written with it on the board, seemingly in no particular or perceptible order – 1412, 1936, 1536, 1965, 1282 – and then duplicated again and again and again, in different sequences, on every square inch of the board, like a random calculation with no apparent conclusion, a mathematical proof proving nothing but the furious desire to prove. And behind these newly scrawled numbers are their own faint and penumbral ghosts, the smudged and partially erased remnants of themselves. Seeing that I have noticed them, Miss Roberts goes to rub them off, and then it comes back to me – the chalk dust on Mr Jones's jacket today. It was there on his shoulders and lapels and sleeves. And so he must be their author. And this is why Miss Roberts comes. Not to keep an eye on the place but to keep an eye on him; to be here with him as he writes and rewrites these numbers, augmenting with each stroke this hoard of spent dust, with no one to see them but the woman he's spent forty years not seeing.

'Well,' she says, and I can hear the unease in her voice, 'I'd really best be off now, boys.'

But Ricky asks would it be OK for us to stay a few more minutes. So many memories, he says. And this the last time we'll get to see the place and everything. His brows come together, sadly, thoughtfully, pleadingly; his head nodding gently with the pity of it, like he might start crying again. Miss Roberts looks pensively about the room, as though it's a terminal patient whose visitors have arrived after the proper hours, and then back at Ricky.

'I suppose it wouldn't hurt, would it? But remember to close the door after you, boys. They come from so far these days, you know, just to steal. They took a television right out of Mrs Pritchard's front room. They'll take anything they can get their hands on.'

Ricky assures her he'll shut the door. He assures her so vehemently it's like he's going to offer to chase them all back single-handedly over the straits, tearing down the bridge as he goes.

'It's been such a pleasure,' she says.

'Hasn't it?' we say.

'Such a shame though, boys, for it to end like this.'

'Isn't it?' we say. Ricky's feet have started shuffling impatiently. He hides them by edging behind a desk.

'Oh, and nice to meet you,' she says to Steph, giving her one last worried glance as she finally turns away.

And then there's just the three of us in the room.

Ricky hardly bothers to wait for Miss Roberts to get on to the road before kicking over the desk in front of him. As it hits the floor the dust explodes, leaping up as if it'd been wanting to all along. Then Ricky moves on to the next desk, and then the next, sending them each toppling over in their turn. And despite the violence of his actions, there's something deliberate, almost graceful, about the way he moves around the room, something almost choreographed about the desks falling in his wake, like in those television montages of condemned buildings being dynamited and collapsing to the soundtrack of a waltz. The dust is thick and alive around us. I can taste its dry, chalky bitterness. Steph's shouting something at Ricky but he can't hear it. His face is set, not in anger or fury, but in a strange, calm, tranced concentration. He finishes with the desks and moves on towards the walls, pulling the bookshelves on to the floor, scattering the trays, and then tearing down the old crayon drawings and the posters. The last one is of the island. It has 'Mon: Mam Cymru' written on the top and pictures of saints and princes drifting around its coasts, afloat in a paper sea. In its centre a mummified fly clings to the fading green of the paper earth.

Once he's finished with the walls, Ricky pauses for a second – I think he smiles – and then rips the black canvas of the board in half. Its torn edges curl backwards, hiding the numbers, and form into two ragged scrolls. Then Ricky picks up a chair and throws it through the window.

The dust spirals over the edges of the broken glass, like

it's escaping from a vacuum, and the outside air pours in. It's as though in this short lapse of time I've forgotten its scent and it surprises me: the smell of fresh earth and grass, the premonitory hint of leaves yet to unfold, the moist, fecund tang of manure. The light that falls through the shattered pane has thickened. It's impossibly bright.

PART SIX

The Coast

Steph

We used to play beachcombers. On the clear days during that winter, the days when we were all together, we'd stalk the coast in search of stuff, anything really, not worried about what we'd find so much as the time we'd lose looking for it. We were killing time, I knew that. We were treading water, waiting for the future to wash up new games, new pursuits, and these were just motions to go through because we'd gone through them before. It was just like the coyote in the cartoon, wheeling his legs around for a second or two before he realizes the ground has disappeared beneath him. Or at least it was for the others. They'd always done this. I hadn't. It was their game. And they didn't seem to realize they'd grown out of it. But I was from town. I was at least two miles older than them. If I'd had other friends I wouldn't have been there.

Most of the time we found nothing really. We'd usually start out from the beach nearest town – where they'd have to collect me – which at high tide was narrow and stony, pinched between the sea wall and the waves, but when the tide let it go spread out into a dark plain of mud that reeked of salt and seaweed and shit and caught hold of rubbish like flypaper: oil drums, pieces of wood, mysterious chunks of Styrofoam, frayed lengths of rope, buoys that had abandoned their moorings, indeterminate lumps of sludge, aquatic molehills. It was all rubbish, and rubbish gets a lot less interesting as you get older. Occasionally Ricky and Del would wade out to pick at something. Neil spent most of his time well above the tideline. Once we found a bike, almost new, which was standing upright in the mud as though its rider had gone over the handlebars. I don't remember what we did with it. We never found the rider, but further along the coast we did find lots of other bodies.

Mostly they were just birds and fish. I didn't know their names but the others would tell me them: gulls, terns, oyster-catchers, cormorants; dogfish, mackerel, bass, sea trout. But occasionally others would turn up. Once we found a brown potato sack which was full of puppies, black and white ones that slithered unseeing out of the sack like small, fat, piebald eels. Their eyelids were closed – I suppose they'd never had a chance to open – and Ricky picked one up and threw it against a rock. Its stomach split open and a tiny crab crawled out.

Another time we found a seal. It was flopped on the sand as if it were dozing there, and at first we were a bit tentative about approaching too close. Eventually Ricky chucked a stone at it and then Del went up and poked it with her stick. It didn't move. It looked too heavy ever to move, ever to have moved, as though tossed out of its element and life it had taken on an unimaginable density and weight. A dead weight. Its eyelids were open, although the gulls had already taken out its eyeballs. Del and Ricky seemed to think this quite a prize and mulled around the body, kicking and prod-ding it, while from further up the beach Neil stared on with a kind of frozen dread, like a swimmer watching the sharks below his feet tearing at a carcass. Ricky wanted to cut its head off for the skull and began hacking at its neck with his penknife, but the skin was too thick and rubbery to cut through. I don't know why he wanted the skull. I knew he wore a gold bear's claw on a piece of string around his neck, but what could you do with a seal's skull? Ricky was always talking about that bear. He told me he'd been in a circus or something with his dad; that they'd come from Russia or somewhere, and had gone back there as well, as far as I could make out. But he never talked about either of them when the others were with us. And when I asked my dad he said Ricky's dad didn't come from Russia, in fact he didn't come from anywhere in particular, and where he'd gone was anybody's guess. As for the bear, he couldn't remember anything about a bear, but if Ricky's dad had kept a pet it probably would have been a snake or a rat or something equally as shifty as him. When Ricky finally managed to make a small puncture in the seal's skin I could smell it from at least ten feet away. It was putrid beyond belief, a heavy, rotten, fishy stench that the sea breeze could do nothing to dispel or disperse. It's a smell that I've never forgotten and it comes back to me sometimes – in the alleyways behind restaurants, from the filthy banks of the Thames, on those hot and stagnant summer days when the drains send their scent into the upper air of the city streets – but never with the concentrated and vivid reek it had that day, when it seemed to hold within it the distilled decay of whole oceans, underwater beds heaped with millions on millions of broken fins and shed scales and barnacled skeletons.

And so that was how it usually went, our beachcombing: the four of us strand-looping for corpses under the winter sun.

It wasn't until much later, the beginning of April, that we found anything more interesting. We'd walked for miles along the coast, drinking a bottle of sherry Ricky had stolen from his mum, which made us self-consciously manic and reflective at the same time, that stop-and-start tipsy you get when you're a kid, waiting for effects you're not sure of but are eager to show off. We'd walk a few feet and then break out into careering circles on the sand, our laughing slightly shrill at first – hyperactive, exaggerated – and then falling into breathless gulps and silence as we checked to see if the wobble in our legs was the dizziness of movement or the dizziness of drink. But the sherry must have been working in some way because even in recollection there seems a disjointedness about our progress, a ragged, almost episodic quality that has us jumping from a sandy cove on to the top of a rocky headland, and then again on to a quarry's edge and the side of a red sandstone cliff, with no notion or sense of having passed through the intervening spaces. And this continues through the whole of that journey, as though we're leaping from frame to frame along a movie reel or flicking through a picture album. It spins us apart. Sometimes I'm only with Del, trying to hold her back while the others go ahead, falling playfully with her on to the sand and my arm lingering around her waist, moving close behind her on a path surrounded by scratchy clumps of bracken. Sometimes I'm only with Ricky, who's trying to hold me back, who attempts to touch my hand beneath a tree bent permanently sideways by the wind. Sometimes Neil is there – Neil who's not drunk anything – watching us reproachfully. Or is he only watching me? And mixed in with this flitting, drunk, disordered sequence there is also a sense that other things and scenes are closer to the surface, breaking through into the fabric of these moments from the past and the future. Ricky's face on my bed, the Candyman's hands, the sight of Del stuck in the window.

And then one final bound has us standing on the white stones of a beach that, after a few seconds, I realize is familiar. The island surprises me again, as it did when me and Del came here before, from landward; although this time it seems to lurch into view like it's been drinking sherry too. The lighthouse sways and totters and its bell slurs out its chimes.

We've not been combing very well. We've found nothing.

We've not even been looking, not really. But now Del begins to concentrate again, moving her stick carefully over the flotsam and jetsam bunched on the tideline, feeling with it, like some bulky ocean bottom-feeder with its antennae, rummaging through the plastic bottles and tin cans, among washed-up branches festooned and swagged with canopies of seaweed. She appears to be concentrating so hard that it's like a rebuke to the rest of us, and we fall in line, sobering up, stooping down on either side of her to search. All of us except Neil, who's gone ahead and is standing further up the beach, near the black rocks which fringe it. Del glances up at him and he comes back towards us. But there's nothing to find, not even bodies, and we're about to give up trying when Del suddenly shouts and heaves some branches aside. And beneath them is a boat. We've found a boat.

It's newer than the bike, wrapped like a gift in a piece of green tarpaulin.

Ricky

Well, it made me feel better anyway. From here it's all down-hill, down to the coast, which is never far away. Sometimes you'll reckon you're miles off it, but it'll always be there, lurking round some corner, just over the next hill, clinging to the next horizon. You're never really on dry land when you're on an island. You may start thinking you are, you may get it into your head that your feet are tramping on the old terra firma, but don't kid yourself – that sea's all around and it's not given up hope of getting back over too. And so whether you think it or not, you'll always have one foot in the water, more or less.

When we were kids we were half fucking amphibian, I swear. We spent so much time on the coast. It was like the island was making it up to us. You've got to live in this village and it's getting smaller every year you get older, and you're beginning to notice you've not got shops that aren't Spar, or cinemas, or pubs that don't know how old you are, or anything else you've started imagining are everywhere on the mainland, and so the island gives you a whole sea instead. There you are, it says, that should keep you going for a bit. And fair dos, it did too. That sea was like our Santa Claus when we were growing up. You just never knew what it'd bring you.

And it seems so stupid now how excited we got to find crap. But crap's different when you're young: it's like treas-

ure or something, like booze and fags are going to be later.
Take a seagull's egg. It's nothing, is it – a big greeny-brown
egg – but fuck, Del and I almost broke our necks a hundred
times climbing up the cliffs for them. She was better at it than
me, nimble as a goat. I reckon I must've had a thing about
heights, 'cause when I couldn't find a hold or a big enough
ledge I'd get all frozen and limpity on the rock face. And then
after a bit I'd start thawing, in a bad way, like the bones were
beginning to drip out of my legs and I was standing on these
empty, wobbly Mr Freeze packets. And the gulls'd be going
nuts around me, which was understandable I suppose, seeing
as I was trying to nick their children. And there'd be Del, way
up above me, monkeying up the cliff like her hands and feet
were covered in Velcro. And because she made it look not
just like she wouldn't fall, but that it was absolutely impossible *to* fall, well, that'd make me start up again, as if she'd
somehow convinced me that gravity was really some kind of
pathetic cry-baby rumour. All that for an egg or two. And
when we'd got them what do we do – we chuck them right
back off the cliff!

It was the same with everything. We'd walk frigging miles
to find pieces of rope and dead birds and all sorts. Honestly,
there can't be much of this coast I've not traipsed along,
holding my breath at the prospect of coming upon a tin can
from America or a Japanese crisp packet. But it is different
then, it really is. That dead bird, well, for a minute or two it's
an almighty wonder. You poke it and prod it as if you've just
discovered a new species and not the same fucker you've seen
a million times in the air above you. Everything from the sea's
booty. We're all wreckers and pirates at heart, and when
you're a kid you can't hide it.

So why does it have to change? Why shouldn't I still be
able to get my kicks rummaging round beaches and estuary
banks, apart from the fact I'd look like the saddest weirdo in

the world? And the worst thing's that I know when it started changing too. Almost exactly. When I was coming over the bridge today it struck me that my life this far is really a before and after thing, it's got a BC and an AD, a split where on one side an egg is worth plummeting off a cliff for and on the other it's just a fucking egg; a dead bird's just a dead bird. And if you've got one of these calendar sort of moments in your life you'll know what I mean, and you'll know how everything seems to be building up and down, towards and away, from that moment, like it's the plug that charges all the electricity in your head and everything that's near it seems bigger, brighter, clearer, more visible, even when you don't want it to be. It's BC and AD, and it's AC and DC too.

So that winter when Steph was around is still lit up in Christmas lights for me, though Christ knows there wasn't anything under the tree. There were these little changes all along, these tremor ones, and they'd mean fuck all usually, you'd never notice them or remember them, except that in the glare of that light it's like you're seeing and remembering through a telescope, through lenses a whole bunch thicker than Del's were even.

For a start Del began going off without us. And I know I'm a fine one to talk, Ricky with his 'Nah, I've got to go home' bollocks, only it seemed different with Del. It's hard to explain. But Del had always kind of taken us under her wing, Neil and me. And looking back, here's me making out Neil was a hopeless case when to be honest I wasn't much fucking better to begin with. I had a bit of hard time myself, not from pissing myself or nothing mind you, but 'cause of my dad I suppose.

'What you got there, Ricky? Better check your pockets, lads.'

'When you going to wash your face, Ricky?'

'Must be frigging hot where you're from, Ricky. You've got a scorching, mate.'

Blah-de-fucking-blah, ha ha. And it was just banter and that but I'd go mad with it, at the start, yeh, lashing out and everything; but the lads who did it were the bigger ones and I'd be getting some real fucking pastings. It took a while to learn to go with it. Josh along. Play the pikey. Until it was 'That Ricky, he's all right.' But inside I'd still be seething and I hated being with them and it was Del who I hung out with, who didn't go in for any of that shit, and who kept an eye on me too. And believe me, nobody messed with her, not the bigger lads, not the older girls, nobody – not 'cause she was dead hard or anything but 'cause she didn't seem to care. It was the same as when she was climbing the cliffs, acting like even the *idea* of falling was so absurd you couldn't believe it yourself. And if anyone gave her stick she'd look at them as if to say, 'What the fuck are you doing, what the fuck are you even *thinking*?', like they'd just done something so totally ludicrous that short of pulling down their kecs, putting feathers in their arses and running about the yard, they couldn't have done anything more ludicrous. And off they'd go, cowed, embarrassed, bewildered, like kittens who'd attacked a rhino. I don't know how to explain it, but some people are like that. And I reckon I've only met a couple of them in my whole life. Neil and me were lucky.

That's why it was different when she went off on her own, and that's why you noticed it: you got so used to that wing you felt a bit lost when it wasn't there. I didn't know where she was going at first. But then one day I spotted her and Steph out by Neil's grandparents' place. It seemed a tad strange, seeing the two of them alone together like that, 'cause I couldn't work out if they even liked each other. Or if Steph liked Del, I should say. I mean, she was always asking me stuff about Del when I was at hers, stuff I didn't give a shit about and couldn't answer, and that she'd end up answering herself. Like where she got her clothes. In the market, she'd answer, as if that meant in the bin. Does her mum cut her hair? Obviously, with a pair of sheep shears probably. And on and on as if she was talking to herself and making a list of crap things about Del and why she shouldn't like her. I, as per frigging usual, was superfluous to requirements. But then every chance she had to hang around with us she took it. It was a mystery to me, or it would've been if I'd ever thought about it – I had other stuff on my mind, believe me. Plus I reckoned that Del wouldn't have given a toss what Steph thought anyway. But seeing them together did make me think about it. I don't know why I didn't go over and join them either. It was like I was suddenly angry with the pair of them: Del for not preferring to be with Neil and me, and Steph for not preferring to be with me, full stop. And so off I go in a huff, with this image of them laughing together in my head and me not even in the picture, in fact me in another picture altogether – twiddling my thumbs alone somewhere in Loserville. And that started changing things.

Then another time I'd been in the mansion, doing my other stint at hopeless causes, and on my way back I catch Del coming out of the Candyman's. Just her. And she's loaded up with this big bag of swag, enough to give a small country diabetes. This time there's a proper reason I don't join her: I don't want anyone to know that I come here. You see, I'm old enough to have figured out that what I'm doing is stupid, pointless, borderline doolally, but I can't stop doing it. If anything I'm getting worse. Because I'm not daft, and I'm beginning to figure out why my mum looks at me like she does. It's because she thinks I'm him. My dad.

I'm used to her blubbing at me, I've been used to it for ever. Most of the time it's over nothing. A rip in my kecs:

'Ricky, why have you done that? They're almost new, sob, sob.' An hour late here or there: 'Why do you do it, Ricky? Why? All I ask is you get back by six . . . blub, blub.' Etc., etc. But now she's angry with me too, all the time, and every inch I get bigger she gets angrier. It's one of them catch twenty-two things. If I'm at home she stares at me as if I'm going to make her puke, and everything I do drives her into a frenzy: leave the top off the marmalade and it's like I've massacred a village of innocents, switch one of her telly programmes over and I've kissed Jesus on the cheek three times. I'm not treading on egg shells, I'm treading on fucking dewdrops. But me staying away makes her as bad. Worse. She'll have the furies the second I sneak in the door. She'll be waiting for me with her speech all prepared: 'This isn't a hotel, Ricky. You treat this place like a fucking hotel, to come and go when you please . . . scream, scream . . . I give up, Ricky. You do what you want. Just go. Just leave me be.' And then when I do it's back to square one or zero or whatever. Off on her mad merry-go-round again. And I'm thinking, no wonder my dad did a runner. This shit makes you dizzy. You never know where you are, so away starts looking pretty damn good. But where am I supposed to go? I'd like to live with my nain but the caravan's too small, and she's getting on, so I'm reckoning if I could just find my dad then I'd be sorted. I wouldn't be a hassle or a ball and chain or nothing; we'd travel around together like, the two of us, it'd be a laugh, an adventure. All I've got to do is find him.

That's why I don't go up to Del that day. Because what I'm doing is plain sad, plain desperate, and she knows it as much as I do. But she doesn't have to say it, does she? Only that's a bit later, and for now I'm creeping back up the track towards the mansion so she won't see me.

Then about twenty minutes later Steph comes up the track. Well, she's not coming up the track exactly, she's veering on to it out of the monkey woods like she's lost and doesn't even know it's the track. She kind of magically appears out of the branches, batting them away with her hands as though they're out to get her. And it looks like some of them have got her too 'cause she's ruffled up a bit, hair all over the place and clothes sort of askew. Those monkey branches can be like monkeys, you know, swinging down at you from the canopies when you're not expecting it, giving you the fright and the fear. I've been in them woods enough times; they're worse in the dark. Steph looks like she's been drinking or something. She's staggering about and her eyes are glassy. She's probably been on the Candyman's lager, I'm guessing – he usually gives us a can or two when we go there, to show he's top of the pops, a bit of a cool old-timer – and then I'm pissed about that too: Steph and Del swigging away in there while I'm picking through crap in the mansion, Sherlock Dickhead; probably knowing I'm there as well, and Del telling them why and them laughing and Steph going, thank fuck I didn't let a freak like that near me.

So when I go up to Steph I'm hardly feeling like Prince Charming, come to cut through the branches and brambles to get her out of here. Or even to point her in the right direction for that matter – 'cause she's heading in the wrong one. She hardly sees me at first and when she does she looks at me like she barely knows me. But that's OK 'cause I'm putting the frost on myself, thinking of them laughing at me in there and Del and her sniggering about me in that hay barn. Lord Ricky the try-hard, Ricky the desperate.

'A-right,' I say. Cold as the driven snow.

And she carries on staring at me like I've bundled in on a day trip from Mars. Well, two can play at that.

'Been out and about, yeh. Just seen Del, we're off to town later.'

And that'll just be us I'm meaning. Not you. Just us old

mates. But the problem with tryng to make people you like upset and jealous is that half the time they don't really get what you're on about. If you're obvious about it then you'll come off as a wanker, but if you're not then they won't get what you're saying at all; they'll take you literally and it won't sound like anything more than passing the time of day. But it doesn't even seem to be sounding like that to Steph. She keeps staring at me.

'Might stay in the village though. Go see Neil and that, Del and me.'

What I'm hoping for is 'I'll come along' or 'What time you meeting?' or something like that, and then me being able to get cagey and say suppose, maybe . . . ummm, ahhh. But I don't get that. What I get is: 'She left me there.'

And then again.

'She left me there.'

I'm not too sure what I'm supposed to do with this. It's not giving me much to work with. And all of a sudden the part of me that likes Steph is switching back from pissed off to wanting again and they're so fucking close together anyway, which you don't know then, do you? I mean, how the hell are you meant to know that hating someone is right there beside liking them, and you're never sure which is which – it's like seeing a tranny-looking bird and wondering what's beneath her skirt. And of course in the end I go down like a pack of cards, go soft and warm as a sunbeam.

'Yeh, I know, Steph. I saw her leaving a while back.' And seeing as she's a bit flustered 'cause she doesn't know her way back properly, I play the gent: 'Look, I'm heading back myself now, might as well stroll via town like. You coming?'

And fuck knows what I've done but she looks at me as if I'm the best beast in jungle, the nicest bloke in the world, as if I've just carried her out of a burning building. Prince Charming it is then, and off we go to hers for my rightful reward, my purse of gold coins. But when we get there nothing's changed. In fact if anything she's even further away on that duvet than before, bunched up with her arms around her knees, staring moodily out the window, behaving like I've got an infectious disease. If I wasn't used to it I'd of been crawling up the walls, but as it is I go through my normal routine of I give up I'm not even going to try next time, no, this is the last time, definitely the last, nothing's going to change on this front. Except that when I say ta-ra and make my usual defeated trudge to the door she leaps up and says, 'Thanks Ricky,' as though I've done her some huge favour or bought her diamonds or something. 'Thanks, Ricky.' And then she plants a big wet smacker right on my gob and I walk out of there reeling, thinking, don't think, Ricky, 'cause if you do you'll never work this shit out. One minute nothing changes and the next everything has.

Because it had. Maybe I hadn't been noticing before – the plug in my head hadn't been switched on yet – but for a while it'd been like the less Steph wanted to do something then the more Del did. It was small stuff mainly. Where we'd go, what we'd do, nothing important, nothing that mattered to Neil and me – we'd be happy doing whatever – but it did to them. Steph was always blathering about going to new places, places we'd not really been together, like the mainland. And Del wanted to hang out where we'd always done, do the stuff we were used to – the three of us. And of course that's what we'd end up doing and Steph'd get the sulks about it. And Christ, none of it meant anything to me, it didn't even cross my radar. But after that day it got much worse and I did notice it. And what I noticed most was that Del was trying, that she was beginning to care about it and you could see it too. And I don't know how to explain this but that sort of knocked me sideways. I'd never seen that in Del. It was like the first time I'd ever seen her falter, like she was up there above me on the cliff face and I'd seen her legs go a bit wobbly, her hands miss a hold, her feet slipping on the rock, and suddenly I did believe in gravity again and was scared shitless of it. And things were suddenly different. Eggs had turned into omelettes and everything seemed a bit broken and I didn't quite know where I was any more or where I was going or what we were looking for.

It was the day before Steph kissed me that we found that stupid frigging boat on the beach. And it was a shit plan, I knew it was then, I knew it was. None of us had a fucking clue what we were doing. We didn't. Honestly.

Neil

Below us the sea runs two ways along the island shore. The tide pulls it in and out over the rocks and sand; but the currents run sideways too. Here, at the edge of the straits, the coasts of the mainland and island splay apart into the stony lips of a hungry mouth and suck the waters into their narrowing throat. At their most constricted point, beneath Telford's bridge, the straits move all ways at once, backwards, forwards, and then around in rippling circles that grow wider and split apart and multiply so that as the tide turns the whole surface whirls and churns and boils as though the water has lost its way and can only make a frantic chase after its own tail. There are old rumours of caves that plunge deep beneath these swirling waters, caves where ancient shipwrecks revolve endlessly and tormented like underwater Sisyphuses, denied for ever the solace of a surface or a shore.

My taid told me about the ships. He liked to tell me ghost stories and he gave them phantom crews, sea-bloated mariners who stared from portholes with the open, unseeing eyes of the drowned, captains trying to steer their wheels with slithery, barnacled hands. His fields are all around us here: Llan Goch on one side, with the earth red beneath its grass; Delyn on the other, with its shape like a harp; and then down to the ones that fringe the sea, Cae Pig and Cael-y-Mor. I wonder if they still have the old names, or if they have names at all now that my taid has left them. Away to our right, behind a copse of hazel and sycamore and plum, is the cottage that isn't his any more, like these fields are no longer his fields. Sometimes the men from the village who come to the George tell me who has bought the cottage, who has bought the fields, as if I needed to be told – as if in some way they will always belong to me – but I can hardly bear to listen.

Outside the kitchen window there was a patch of smoothed earth where my taid's favourite pig, Bill the Boar, used to sleep. He'll eat your hand, my taid would chuckle. Chomp, chomp, his jaws would go, abrupt and greedy in imitation of Bill's. He'll have it off just like that. Chomp, chomp.

Paid, my nain would say. Stop that. You'll frighten him.

I'd look down my arm at my hand, twitch my fingers. How could my hand not be there? How could something be there and then not be there? It wasn't possible. Bill could never steal my hand – it was mine.

You listen to your taid though, Neil bach. You mustn't feed that pig.

Chomp, chomp, his jaws would go, silently, while she wasn't looking. His eyes would still be chuckling. And mine would chuckle back. I'd run my fingers over the table like a spider and his jaws would chase them in skittering circles.

Stop that, my nain would say, smiling as though we were both her children; smiling because she didn't really want us to stop.

Instead of my hand she'd give us a plate of buttered bread to eat. White rectangles with the butter slabbed on top of them. The thick yellow wedges that would get my taid in the end, that would cage him in clotted arteries after he'd managed to escape everything else – even the Japanese army. It was the peril he never saw coming.

'You listen to your taid . . .'

I'd been feeding Bill rose-hips. The hedgerows were bleeding them that autumn. I collected handfuls on the walk from my parents' house to the farm and kept them in my pockets. Sometimes one would break and the itchy seeds would tingle against my thighs. I was five that year, and I think it's the first year I can remember as a whole, with four seasons and no gaps or missing pieces.

Bill ranged free around the farmyard. The other pigs were penned in the field behind it but my taid let Bill wander where he wanted. He rooted about in the yard, lording it over Carlo and Mot, the sheepdogs. He chased Joe the Baker's van until Joe was forced to hurl stale, appeasing buns to him. I think he chose his favourite patch of ground, beneath the kitchen window, to spite my nain. She waged a constant and fruitless campaign to shift him. Usually, as I entered the yard, she'd be leaning out the window, shouting at Bill and prodding his head with a broom, which only seemed to delight him; he'd grunt contentedly as he lay there, twitching the huge ears that half covered his eyes, and shuddering with pleasure as though he were being stroked. Other times she'd pour pots of water over him and he'd turn on to his side and wallow luxuriantly in it. And whatever new schemes my nain devised to move Bill, the more he'd take them as signs of affection and the more firmly and comfortably he'd ensconce himself beneath the window, looking for all the world as if he was slightly surprised she hadn't invited him into the kitchen itself.

My nain's predicament with Bill was a constant theme of conversation in the cottage. 'Look at that mess,' she'd proclaim ruefully as she prepared our bread and butter.

'Look at him there, rolling in his own filth. *Arglwydd*, and the smell of it. Can you smell it, Neil? Of course you can. I wake up with that smell, you know, and I go to bed with it too, Neil. And I probably sleep with it as well, my dreams all stinking of pig filth. Can you imagine it? Can you imagine it? It's like he owns the place.'

And as she spoke she'd glance over reproachfully at my taid, who'd be sitting with me at the table.

'It's good for the earth,' he'd say, smiling at me. We were used to this.

'Oh, and of course there's no other earth around the place for it to be good for! No, no, we've got to have pig shit right here outside our front door. I don't know, Neil, I really don't, why don't you ask your taid what he's planning to grow outside our kitchen window, because that damn pig's eaten everything else that grows. *Esgob*, good earth he says, Neil. Good earth! That's the barest piece of good earth I've ever seen.'

My taid winked at me. 'Maybe Bill's just planting things, eh, Neil?'

'Planting things! The only thing that's going to come from that pig is more filth and more pigs.'

And on and on they'd go. And sometimes I'd get a small pang of guilt when I remembered my own complicity in Bill's sojourn beneath the window, because all through that autumn I kept on feeding him the rose-hips. He never looked like he was going to eat my hand, lying there swatting away the slow, leftover flies of the season with his ears. After a while he came to expect them when he saw me, lifting his head off its pillow of bare earth to watch me approach, snuffling in expectation as I reached into my pockets, staring lazily – but gratefully – at me with his small, short-sighted eyes.

I felt a stronger pang of guilt towards the end of the autumn when Bill fell sick with a fever. I thought it was the rose-hips and admitted to my nain that I'd not stopped feeding him. But she said pigs could eat anything and it wasn't the rose-hips that had made him ill. She said pigs got fevers all the time and it wasn't my fault. And I thought Bill would recover because my taid got fevers all the time too. Every year he'd have to spend a week – sometimes more – in his bed with his fever, which my nain said would never properly leave him because it was called malaria and it stayed with you for ever. She said he'd caught it in Burma during the war and it was like a scar that didn't go away. When he had it he turned yellow and sweated and saw things that weren't there, people, animals, the friends that had not come home with him. He'd talk to them, and occasionally he'd scream and shout at them too. Afterwards, when he was feeling better, I'd ask him who he'd been talking to, who he'd seen. And he said he was speaking to ghosts. He said that the dead were never far away from us, that they only ever played a kind of hide and seek with the living, choosing their moments to reveal themselves, and that when he had his fever he could see them all around him. They forget nothing, he said. Nothing. And sometimes they would go over old memories with him, and old argu- ments too – arguments that could never be finished or resolved or made up because only the living can do that.

But Bill's fever wasn't like my taid's fever. They brought him into the kitchen so he could lie beside the stove, but he showed no enthusiasm over this unexpected triumph over my nain. He stared listlessly at the linoleum and refused to eat the treats my taid pushed in front of his snout. And my nain seemed to take no pleasure in his misfortune either, whisper- ing encouragement into his huge ears – which were now as motionless as rags – when she thought nobody was looking.

My taid took it badly when he died. I didn't quite under- stand why he should be so upset by the death of this one animal. I'd watched him push dead cows off the cliff at the edge of Cael-y-Mor without even a flicker of emotion pass- ing over his face; and when Mot had puppies I'd seen him put them into a brown potato sack and when I'd asked him where he was taking them he'd winked at me and said they were off to join the navy. But with Bill it was different. He kept his body in the kitchen until my nain told him that if he wouldn't move it then she would. And then he said he wanted to bury him under his spot outside the window. My nain baulked at this: she'd had him there long enough when he was living, she said, she wasn't going to have him there dead as well. But my taid was adamant. It was the first time I'd seen them argue properly.

The next day I walked into the yard and found my taid digging below the window. I knew he'd not won the argument because my nain was in our house talking to my mum. It was late in the autumn by then and a heavy drizzle was falling. It had been falling unabated for days, and as I'd walked along the lane to the farm I'd looked at the last leaves on the trees and wondered if in the end they didn't fall at all but were instead corroded away by this drizzle, like the thin strips of rusting iron they now resembled. A year later this thought would come to me again when I watched a programme on television where a man talked about the acid rain that would fall over the world during a nuclear winter. I would dream about this rain. But I hadn't dreamed of it yet when my taid handed me a trowel – I wasn't big enough to hold a spade – and let me help him dig Bill's grave. I wasn't much help really. My trowel only got in the way of my taid's spade but he humoured me and it was only years afterwards that it occurred to me that in letting me help he was also enlisting me as a collaborator, was making sure that when my nain returned we'd both have Bill's grave on our hands, and that this would lessen her anger.

The drizzle became heavier as we dug. It settled on my taid's thinning, grey hair, like dew drops on spiders' webs, and then ran down his forehead before dripping into the grave. It gathered in the drains beneath the eaves and fell in cascades on to the ground beside us, before making its inexorable way down into the hole, forming rivulets in its sides and carrying back some of the earth we'd only just taken out.

Before long my taid's spadefuls were as much water as earth, and what he heaved over his shoulder became an arc of muddy spray, like an elephant washing its back at an oasis. 'That's enough,' he said after a while. 'We might as well be digging a hole in the bloody sea.'

He dragged Bill out of the kitchen, which was difficult because his legs had stiffened and wouldn't bend through the door, so we had to push him on to his back and balance him there to get him outside. My taid was in a hurry now. He must have known my nain would be back soon and if he didn't get Bill into the hole before long then he never would. But Bill was as hard to push around when he was dead as he had been when living. His legs caught hold of every obstacle they could reach, the plastic bins, an old aluminium milk churn, two empty flower pots, and left a path of disarray in their wake. Twice he squirmed out of my taid's grasp altogether, sending him sprawling backwards on to his behind. And my taid must have liked him a lot because he got back up without swearing, without anger or frustration even, and carried on dragging him. But I began to sense that Bill didn't want to go into the hole. I'd been trying to push him as my taid pulled, but now I only pretended to – leaning against his haunches without applying any pressure or effort. I started to hope my nain would arrive back early and put a stop to what we were doing. I searched through the drizzle, across the yard and up the track as far as I could see, but she wasn't there. And then Bill was on the edge of the hole and I knew it was too late. My taid gave him a final shove with his foot and he toppled into it, landing on his back, with his legs pushing against its sides.

The water covered half of his body and most of his head. One of his ears floated on its surface like a lily pad, and just at its edge the slightly curved tip of his snout protruded out as though it were trying to follow one last, diminishing scent into the open air, as though Bill's reversal was now almost complete and he was grubbing upwards from the dirt into the sky. I watched as my taid threw spadefuls of mud on to Bill's belly and the water rose. The drizzle had become heavier again and the air itself felt like water, like it was too dense and wet to breathe. And then Bill began to breathe. To begin with I thought it was foam thrown up by the rivulets running down the sides of the hole, but then I could see they were bubbles and that they were coming from beneath the tip of Bill's snout, where his mouth would be. At first they came up slowly, in ones and twos, barely breaking the film of the surface, but then they quickened and multiplied and burst through it. I ran over and grabbed hold of my taid's arm. 'He's breathing,' I shouted, my voice sounding weak in the drizzle. 'He's breathing.'

'He can't breathe, Neil. He's dead.'

'But he is,' I pleaded. 'Look!'

I pointed to the bubbles which were now getting fewer and smaller again. My taid glanced down at them and I was sure he was going to jump into the hole and pull Bill's head above the water. But he didn't.

'That's just gas, Neil,' he said, looking at me sadly. 'It swells up in their bellies when they die.'

I didn't understand what he was talking about.

'But he's breathing,' I shouted, desperately now because there were hardly any bubbles left. They were coming up in ones and twos and the intervals between were getting longer and longer.

'That's not breath, Neil,' he said. 'That's air.'

But air was breath. How could air not be breath? 'He's dying,' I cried. 'You're letting him die.'

'He's dead already, Neil,' my taid said, slowly and quietly. And suddenly he looked tired, more tired than I had ever seen him, standing gaunt and soaked in the drizzle that felt like it would never stop. I looked on as the last bubbles flopped to the surface.

The ground under the window remained bare all through that winter, a muddy affront to my nain; a sign, so she would have it, that my taid was going soft or mad or both. But I could hardly look at it. I imagined Bill still there beneath the slowly receding bulge of the earth, gasping in his grave of brown and stagnant water; a grave which I thought could not evaporate because the sun couldn't reach it. When my taid stood on top of it to repair the window frame, I saw the water ooze out of the earth and gather around the soles of his boots, and I was sure it was the same water, trickled from his inundated lungs. My father, who was more sentimental than his parents – or had become so after moving to the village – tried to tell me that animals went up to heaven, even pigs, but I wasn't going to believe that. When I pictured Bill, I pictured him going down – tumbled blackly along in underground rivers and cataracts, through inky reservoirs, and finally into dark, silent pools that the light had never seen, where blind, translucent creatures would caress him with their feelers.

That spring a green shoot appeared beneath the window. All through the season it crept further up, hugging the wall, uncurling small green tendrils over the stone.

'I told you he was good for the earth,' I heard my taid say.

'Well, he is now,' my nain replied.

By the summer it had risen almost a foot.

That same summer my mother tried to teach me to swim. She took me to the beach by my taid's fields and sat me on the white stones in front of the lighthouse and the island. She waited for high tide because when the tide was low the stones further down the beach were slippery and difficult to walk over. I didn't want to go in.

She pulled me to the water's edge and put her own feet in the water to show me it was all right. It's not even cold, she said. She was wearing a green bathing suit and her skin was almost whiter than the stones. There were freckles on her arms and across her nose. Her ribs jutted out from her sides as she took a deep intake of breath against the coolness of the water. I knew it was cold. I could see the goose-pimples spreading up her thin legs. I wouldn't put my feet in. At first she was exasperated and tried to pull me towards her, but I sat down on the stones and held on to them. Then she relented and cupped her hand around my head and ruffled my hair at the back, caressed it at the sides. Her fingers felt cool and safe and smooth like the stones. 'It's fine,' she said. 'Look, it's fine,' she said, walking away from me into the water. She waded through it until it was up past her thighs and then paused for a second, holding her hands together over her belly, the top half of her body swaying slightly and her shoulders hunched against her neck, before falling forwards and disappearing. For a second she was gone. The swell quietly lapped the shore and two gulls hovered in circles above me. It seemed so lonely on the beach that suddenly I wished I'd gone into the water with her. And then she reappeared, bobbing up through the surface with a gasp a few yards from where she'd gone in, bringing her hands up to her face to wipe her eyes and push back her hair.

'See,' she called to me. 'It's lovely. Why don't you come in? Just a little bit, just up to your knees.'

I wouldn't move. Her strawberry hair had turned dark and her face was red, so you could hardly notice the freckles. She wore a necklace. I think she wore a necklace.

Because I wouldn't move she swam further out. She went out past the black rocks on either side of the beach, towards the straits and the lighthouse. The gulls followed her, swooping lower and lower. I knew she shouldn't go near the lighthouse. I knew she shouldn't go past the rocks. My taid had told me how the currents ran sideways here; he'd stood with me in Cael-y-Mor and moved his finger across the sea and into the mouth of the straits and told me how beyond the rocks the currents ripped fast and sideways. He told me about the sailors beneath the bridge.

My mother's head was there and then it wasn't there. And then it was there again. I got up and shouted out to her but she only waved. And then it was gone again. Apart from the cries of the gulls it was quiet. I wished I was with her out there in the water. I had never felt so alone. When her head came back again I ran across the beach and climbed up on to the rocks, shouting and shouting. I was crying too. My face was hot and stinging. And then she was near the rocks and I was running along the beach, tripping on the stones.

When she picked me up the water dripped from her body and soaked into my tee-shirt. She held me against her and her skin was cold and clammy. She brushed the hair back from my forehead.

'It's OK,' she said. 'It's OK now. I'm here.'

But she hadn't been there when she was in the water. Where had she been when I couldn't see her? I wouldn't let go of her until we were away from the beach.

By the next spring the plant had grown up almost to the window's ledge. It had tiny thorns which hadn't quite hardened yet.

'I told you he was good for the earth,' my taid proclaimed.

But my nain didn't say anything because my mother was ill.

She'd been ill all through the winter. There were green arrows on the floor of the hospital corridor when we went to see her. I can remember them. Everything else in the hospital seems to have been swallowed up in a kind of white glare, a sharp, disinfected, enamel surface that reflects nothing back, no objects, no faces, no pictures, no colours, nothing but its own blank whiteness. Outside of that whiteness I am always sitting in my nain and taid's kitchen. I'm never at home. In front of me there's anything that I want, doughnuts, sweets, crisps, and bags my nain has brought from the hospital, full of Lucozade bottles and shrivelled apples and grapes. My father isn't there; he has become part of the whiteness as well somehow – though he flits in and out of it, appearing in the yard occasionally, or walking through the fields with my taid. People from the village come in and out of the kitchen and speak too softly for me to hear.

And then I am at home. And the people from the village are there too, speaking just as softly. The drizzle is there as well. It has fallen all through the morning and the cars outside have their wipers on. When we drive the short distance to the chapel, the wheels slop through puddles and outside the window the sky isn't visible, only the drizzle, which a slight breeze has formed into airy sheets which billow past one after the other, scattering on to the glass and running down it in patterns, blurring the faint colours of the spring leaves on the hedges and trees and wetting their bark, until they appear blackened and charred and I think again of acid rain, of that moisture which sears and burns and will one day fall over all the world.

In the yard the water flowed over my new shoes. They were made of shiny black leather, stiff and unyielding, cramping and scraping my toes. It crept in through the holes for the laces and then forced its way over their tongues. I studied its progress, only vaguely aware of a voice that had begun to rise and fall above me, a sea-swell of a voice that had caught my mother's name and toyed with it, bobbing it up and down on the surge and retreat of its syllables so that one moment it was there and the next it wasn't. Up and down it went, appearing and disappearing, until finally it had vanished altogether; the voice closing over it like it never been there at all. I looked past the front of my shoes and down into the hole that gaped just beyond them. I looked at the box that they said was my mother, watching the muddy water rise over the wet, dark wood, waiting for the bubbles that didn't come. I watched it approach the edge of the lid, and then my mouth opened, forming a wide silent 'o', out of which nothing came either, not a single sound.

Two weeks later a flower opened on the plant. It was a light, delicate pink. It's a rose, my nain told me. A wild rose.

And I thought Bill would come back then. And I thought she would too.

PART SEVEN

The Island

Steph

Del peels back the tarpaulin and inside we find two oars, a coil of rope, a pair of waterproof leggings, a bucket and a child's plastic spade. It's not much, nothing to get excited about, but Ricky tries his best; he takes out the leggings, puts them on, and then grabs an oar, runs down to the shoreline and bats a stone into the water. He attempts to hit another one but the oar's too long and heavy and by the time he manages his lumbering swing the stone's already hit the ground. He bursts out laughing and swings the oar in a full circle, spinning around until he slips on some seaweed and topples down. He thinks we're laughing with him but we're not. The helter-skelter momentum that carried us here has dwindled now; everything's slowed down and Ricky suddenly appears a bit stupid and out of place, the last one to leave the party. A flock of small birds glide past over the sea, following each other so carefully and closely that they look like one giant, shape-shifting bird whose feathers continually flicker, white and brown and brown and white. The sluggish heave of the flat, oily water, the ponderous chimes of the lighthouse bell, the lazy, curving drift of the gulls through the air – all of them seem synchronized somehow, in time, and with the sherry fading we've fallen into that time too. Eventually Ricky throws the oar aside and trudges sheepishly back towards the boat.

For a while we just lean on its sides, staring into its bottom as if something more interesting is going to appear there.

'Stupid place to keep a boat,' Ricky says half-heartedly. 'Anybody could nick it.'

'Let's go,' says Neil. 'There's nothing in it.'

'I reckon it's that lobster bloke's,' Ricky says. 'You know, that one who's got them pots in town. If we could get one of them pots . . .'

Del's looking at me. She's been looking at me since she found the boat. I don't know what she wants. The sun hangs listlessly above us in the sky and it makes me feel sleepy and bored and sad. I'm disappointed and I don't really know why; but it's there in my stomach as though in the blurred rush here something's been lost and there's no way of scrabbling back to find it. I can see a yacht becalmed in the distance and I think of my duvet at home, the soft touch of its cotton. I've had enough of beachcombing.

'If we could get some of them pots . . .' Ricky says but I can barely hear him. I can't be bothered to listen to this kids' stuff any more. I've had enough of him as well.

'Let's go,' says Neil to nobody in particular, and nobody listens.

'We can take it to the island,' Del says, looking at me.

'I'm going home,' I say.

'We could get there easily.'

'You lot can do what you like. I'm going home.'

'You don't have to come,' she says. And she says it so dismissively that suddenly I'd like to slap her. A fragment comes back to me from before, of her pushing me away as I cling to her on the sand, and the ache comes into my stomach again. She's looking at the boys now. Neil looks down at his feet. Ricky doesn't know where to look. He wants to look at me.

The island is closer than before. In just a few weeks its

cliffs have shrunk and the strip of water between it and the shore has lessened. She's so slippery, she's so hard to get a hold of, but even now I can't stop trying. And I'm still following her. Before I know it I'm making plans to meet them here when I know going to the island means nothing to me, when I know it shouldn't matter what Del thinks of me, when I should be walking away.

Ricky

There it is then, ahead of us – Seiriol's Island – with its cliffs and rocks and tiny hermit's tower. If it wasn't enough us living on one big island we had to have these little ones around it too, a bunch of them scattered up and down the coast as if when the world was being made God sort of lost the plot or the energy when he got to us and started flinging what he had left all over the place, like he was making a jigsaw and got bored with it and left a load of pieces lying about around the edges. Apparently God folk have always loved these islands; and wouldn't that be like them too, getting it into their heads that the Almighty hadn't got tired with the effort of it all but had made these islands just for them instead?

This one's Seiriol's, who was our saint. We've all got a saint round these parts, every town, every village, every other tree or field too, it seems sometimes. You must've been nothing without one back in the day. It must've been like having Sky or cable – if you didn't have a saint then you weren't connected to the Bigger Picture and you didn't get the best programmes; you were just a bunch of hicks who thought heaven was a good harvest and God and Jesus drank in the local on Saturday nights and pulled off miracles with dominoes and darts. You needed your saint to tell you about blinding white lights and ineffable glories and choirs of angels and all that malarky.

Mr Jones used to tell us about Seiriol. How he had this mate called Cybi – a saint as well, would you believe it? – who lived on the opposite side of the island, and that he'd go meet him every day for a chat about how they were getting on converting the pagans or whatever. And because they were both reasonable blokes, being saints and everything, they'd always meet halfway, in the middle of the big island, and not on their own little ones – of course Cybi had his as well. Now it was a bit of a trek for the pair of them. They'd have set off first thing in the morning if they were going to make it for lunch – unless they were fasting – and so Cybi was always walking into the sun 'cause he lived on the west side, and Seiriol was always walking away from it 'cause he was from the east side. Anyway, the upshot of the whole story was that Cybi got a hell of a tan on him from this so they called him Cybi Felyn, and Seiriol stayed as pale as a sheet so they called him Seiriol Wyn. And I remember this 'cause at the time I'd be thinking that if Mr Jones is making out that this Cybi's so frigging holy and wonderful and dutiful with his tan, then what's he got against me and my dad? Nobody here's looking at my face like it's a gift from above, browned by the reflected gleam of God's toothy white smile.

But I'm remembering this story now 'cause when he told us it then it never occurred to me how Seiriol got off his island in the first place, let alone back on it. Maybe God made it easy for him, let him walk on water, or parted them for him. But that'd be a lot of miracles. I mean, twice a day, that's practically commuting, and you're not supposed to get divine aid for that, are you? Or perhaps he had one of them coracle things. They made one of them once in town, one of those historical groups that dress up as knights and maidens, or Victorian gents and their buxom squeezes, putting on pantos about how peachy it was when we used to live on turnips and gruel and sleep twelve to a bed in a hovel and get our sisters up the duff. Ah, the good old days, when it was all meadows and all that other crap. And that coracle was definitely a piece of crap. They dressed this bloke up as a sailor – jaunty red scarf, cap with an anchor, the whole regalia – and cheered him on his way off the end of the pier, and he gets about five feet across the deep blue when a tiny ripple from some speedboat at least three miles in the distance hits him and over the coracle goes. He might as well have launched himself to sea in an empty margarine tub.

And the fact is, those straits between Seiriol's Island and the shore aren't safe. You can look at them from here and see nothing, a nice shiny, still surface, but underneath the currents are as strong as fuck. There's rip tides and undertows and all sorts of chaos going on down there. So how did Seiriol waltz over them twice a frigging day without even getting his cowl wet? They should have had that in the story. I mean, you're supposed to learn shit from stories, aren't you? Saint meets saint, saint gets tan, saint doesn't get tan, saints end up in heaven – what's that going to teach you? Who's going to put their hand up in careers class and say, actually I've been considering sainthood myself, how might I go about that? Well, I'm glad you've brought that up, young Johnny, I've got a few stories here that might help you on your way, about island residences and miracles and martyrdom and the like; yes, just take the leaflet with you when you go, I can get five thousand of them out of that five. No, it wouldn't have killed them to mention it, to put that saint shit on the back-burner and say those straits are dangerous. God may have been looking out for Seiriol but you lot are hardly at the front of his queue.

We've almost made it, which is handy 'cause I'm losing the heart for this now. When I got that letter from Steph I was gobsmacked, I'll admit, but I reckoned what the hell – a trip back's not going to hurt. It's been ages and everything and I'll be happy to see the old place, I really will. In fact there's me all cocky 'cause for years I've been bringing it up in the pub, how I'm from an island and how great it is; joking around about how there's palm trees everywhere and we never have to wear shoes and we all get about in coracles. And some of the folk half believing me too, 'cause in their heads islands are all a bit like that – paradises full of hula skirts and pina coladas and beach huts with grass roofs – and not pretty much exactly the same as the places where they grew up. And then after a bit I start half believing my shit myself. I'll be blathering away and those palm boughs will be waving and beckoning in *my* head – the white sands will be sparkling under the sun, the gulls will have turned into parrots with beautiful feathers and be winging their way over the deep green fields and coral beds, and I'll be looking out the rain-smeared windows at the pavements and buildings thinking, I wish I was there, I wish I was there more than anything. Christ, sometimes it'll get more than I can handle and I'll feel a blub coming on and have to nip off and hide my eyes in the bogs. It'll be like I've turned my BC into some fucking holiday brochure. And of course I never mention the other stuff, do I, so after a while I must've just thought, it's not there any more, it's not in this picture so it's not in any picture. It's only when I'm alone that the picture changes and I make sure I'm hardly ever alone. I'm friends with half of London Town these days, I'm telling you.

And that surprises me as much as anything when I get Steph's letter: that we're both living here and I've never bumped into her or seen her. You see, you never really get the village thing out of your brain for good. You live in the same place as someone, you expect to meet them. That's there for ever, an instinct. It doesn't matter how many million people live in the new place, or how big it is, your brain's still computing it in village terms. And so I start wondering if I have seen her but didn't clock it. I mean, she's got to look different and I've not set eyes on her face since I tore up that poster her dad gave me. And for the weeks before coming here I find myself staring at faces – in pubs, on the Underground, in parks, anywhere I happen to be – thinking maybe it's her. The strange thing's that every time I do think maybe, there's this little jolt in my stomach and I don't know what it is or what it's about, except that it's familiar some-how. And it's only now that it's hit me.

That's what I felt like when I was looking for my dad. That jolt. That maybe. That 'it could be' feeling when obviously it's fucking impossible. And do you know, it was familiar 'cause I've never stopped doing it, not once, not for one second of one frigging day whether I think I'm doing it or not. Everywhere I've been – and I've been to a lot of places – my eyes linger on people just that moment more than they need to, that moment more than anyone else's, following them in doors, round corners, across the street. And for what? To recognize a face that I always reckoned would be exactly like my own anyway, like me in the mirror, as if time wouldn't have changed it a jot, as if an old fucking photo I don't even have 'cause my mum chucked it away is going to come to life and plod down the street and say, hey, that's me in the mirror too, would you believe it? Must be Ricky! And without noticing it, it's like I'm doing some kind of sum in my head – one down, three fucking billion to go – a sudden, hopeless subtraction that makes me feel a little bit less than I did the second before but that I can't stop doing.

Del never had to say it though, did she? It was nothing but she didn't have to. We were sitting in the shelter, just me and her, and it was a beautiful day. Really beautiful. I remem-ber that. Sun, no wind, and that spring freshness they always say is going to be in cans of spray or things to hang in cars but never is. Maybe the palms were swaying and the sands were sparkling and the parrots were flying too, I don't know, but I was feeling pretty damn good about the world. I still had the feel of Steph's lips on me from a couple of days before, which was kind of a taster I was reckoning, a hint of things to come. The lights seemed to be changing on that front and it made it feel like all the other fronts were the same. Everything was turning green: the trees, the fields, the hedges, the lot. It was all go. And I'm looking at the bus timetable outside the shelter, thinking that I might as well sort the lot out at once.

'I'm going to Chester,' I tell Del.

'Why?' she asks. And that's a tricky one. Because I heard two blokes in town talking about a caravan site full of pikeys outside Chester. Because I'm on a roll and everything is green and possible. Because it's time to move on from the mansion and my mum and everything.

'Dunno, 'cause.'

'You're not going to find him.'

'Who?'

'Your dad.'

She didn't have to say anything. She never had before and I'd loved her for that: knowing but never saying. And I can't work out what made her say it then. I've gone over this a thousand times and I can't understand it. She sat there look-ing like she'd said nothing, like she'd just said, 'Nice day this, eh, Ricky?' But she must have known it mattered to me. She must have known my guts were twisting and they were too, they were writhing, and suddenly the palms had gone and the sands were all shit dunes and the parrots were these rat-faced gulls laughing at me with their screechy, squawky laughs. Ricky the village idiot. And you'd never made me feel like that, Del. Never. I've gone over and over this a thousand times and it keeps getting bigger and smaller. I can see from here that maybe it *was* nothing, but I can also see how it's

going to become something – it's like that butterfly stuff they
talk about, the flap and the hurricane. But fuck the butterflies, isn't that just like islands for you: making things seem
bigger and smaller at the same time, making stuff seem close
and far away, making them straits look harmless when they're
not?

Neil

Del pretended to find the boat and I didn't know why she did that. She took the branches off it and pretended to look surprised and Del didn't ever pretend things. I thought she didn't need to. She'd never hidden anything before, not from Ricky or me or anyone. It was only when Steph was there that she started to. We didn't have secrets until Steph was with us.

The others had been drinking sherry. On the way here they'd been running and stopping, laughing and going quiet, splitting apart and then coming back together. As I'd watched a flock of dunlins and turnstones had seemed to follow them, sweeping along the shoreline and mimicking them; spinning in giddy, gliding circles, flickering white then brown then white, separating and spiralling like strands of smoke and then merging again like bee swarms. They followed them all the way to the boat before settling almost invisibly among the stones. Sometimes Del was with Steph and sometimes Ricky was with Steph. And I didn't want anyone to be with Steph. I wanted it to be like it had been before, with only the three of us. I wanted Del to be with me.

I'd seen Del's face that night in the Robinsons' and I couldn't understand why she still wanted Steph to be around. But Ricky told me he'd seen them hanging out together at the Candyman's and when I thought about that I hated Steph again.

We were going to go to Seiriol's Island. Steph said she didn't want to but when Del said we were going to go anyway then she said she did want to.

The island didn't seem far away but I didn't look at it. The Candyman had told us he used to own the island. There were pictures of it in his cottage that he said some of his relatives had drawn, two spinster sisters who drew everything – flowers and plants and cliffs and islands. I tried to think of their islands instead of this one, done in dry ink and held behind glass.

I thought we were going to go right away, and maybe we would have, but a group of old people had appeared on the road that came down to the beach. We hid the boat again, under the branches and seaweed, even though they wouldn't have seen it anyway. They'd stopped opposite the lighthouse and were staring out towards the island, craning their necks as though their sight couldn't reach that far. I don't think they even saw us. We were as invisible to them as the dunlins and turnstones were, chirruping among the rocks and weeds and shells.

Del said we'd go on Friday and we all said we would. One o'clock on Friday. April 6th.

Steph

Before we reach the beach Neil turns down the track that leads to his grandparents' cottage. I wouldn't recognize it except I have the island as a marker now and for the rest of the way I'll know exactly where I'm going. The barbed wire and the walls that lined the track have gone; they've turned into tidy wooden fences that smell faintly of preserving chemicals. The thistles in the fields have gone. The hay barn is gone too. There's horses in the fields and stables in the yard. A woman in spotless jodhpurs is standing by the door of the cottage, which has a polished brass knocker hanging on it. The windows of the cottage have grown into a glass conservatory and the bushes around them have shrunk into little plants in pots. They sit on the paving stones that now circle it.

Halfway down the track Ricky turns to Neil and asks, 'Why are we going here?' He says it listlessly, as though he doesn't care where he's going any more. Neil doesn't say anything. He's looking at the cottage.

The fence around the yard is painted white and has a gate with glistening black hinges. They don't even squeak when Neil pushes it open. The woman's seen us and she's walking across the yard, smiling. Her teeth are as white as the fence.

'Hello there,' she says. 'What can I do for you?'

Neil walks right past her and the smile goes.

'Excuse me!' she says, turning to follow him. 'What

exactly do you want here?' The creases forming on her forehead are the only ones on her. Neil doesn't look back and so
she turns to Ricky and me instead.

'What's going on?' she asks us. 'Who are you?'

'It's a-right,' Ricky tells her. 'This is his grandparents' old
place. Wanted to have a bit of a look, that's all.'

'Why didn't he say? This is private property, you know.'

'He's a-right – just doesn't speak much. Leave him be for
a few minutes and then we'll be off.'

'I could call the police.'

'There's no need for that, is there? Just leave him for a bit.
He's only looking.'

'You can't just walk on to someone else's . . .'

The woman won't shut up. And Ricky's right: Neil's only
looking. He's standing outside the conservatory looking down
at the paving stones.

Neil

When I turned on to the track to my nain and taid's they followed me. And I didn't want them to any more, Del. I only want it to be us now. You and me and not them.

It's all changed, Del. Do you see it the same way I see it? Or do you still see it like it was before? It's gone, Del. They're gone.

Ricky

Police this, police that – who is this woman anyway? I don't recognize her. Look, I tell her, he's come to have a stare at the cottage. Yes, it's a bit weird I admit, but it's harmless. And besides, I'm damn fucking sure you came and gawped at a load of these cottages yourself before you bought this one. And I'll bet no one jumped out the door and started saying stuff about the police. So leave it out and let it be. We'll be off in a second and you won't be seeing us again in a hurry, I promise you that.

And just to help things along I go and try dragging Neil away. 'Come on, mate' I say, 'it's getting on for half one. If you want to be there by then we'd best keep moving.'

'It's gone,' he's saying. And I haven't got a frigging clue what he's on about. He's always been an odd one, Neil, even when we were kids, but I don't remember him this odd. The woman's giving us the evil eye now.

'Leave it out, Neil. We're going to get in trouble here,' I tell him, but he's not shifting. He's gawping down at the paving stone by his feet.

And then he's on his knees and he's scraping at it with his fingers. Great! The evil eye's popping out of its socket now. It's got mental asylum *and* police written on it. Steph's trying to calm her down but what's she going to say? Sorry, my friend would like to dig up your patio with his hands. I'm sure you'll understand. You're new round these parts, but honestly, this is just what we do here. Welcome to the island.

He's a thin little fucker, is Neil. You'd think he would've bulked out a bit after all these years but he hasn't. He's the same old skin and bones. Or the same young ones. When I grab him my hands feel as if they're about to go right through his ribs and come out on the other side. He's squirming about and he's dead hard to keep hold of. There were these films that were always on around this time of year when I was a kid, with mad-looking monsters that were like moving toys with a touch of arthritis, a bit stiff in the joints, yeh. There was a Cyclops, a bird with snakes for hair, a dragon with loads of heads. And there was one of them where this bloke sows some teeth in the ground and all these angry little skeletons grow out of them, waving swords and shields above their skulls. And that's what Neil's like now, except he's only got his hands to thrash around with. I'm not worried about them hitting me. They wouldn't hurt. I'm not proud of this but I used to do this move when we were kids, where I'd rile him up until he tried to hit me and then I'd put my hand on his forehead and let him swing at me, knowing he couldn't quite reach and if he did it wouldn't hurt. No, what I'm worried about is that woman. I'm reckoning she's guessed Neil's not quite right by now, 'cause whatever Steph was saying to her it hasn't worked and she's hot-footing it to the door.

'For fuck's sake, Neil. Pack this in, mate,' I'm telling him. And it's funny but I'm saying it in a whisper, soft and all affectionate like. And I mean it like that too. He may have fallen off the milk float but there's this sudden moment where it's like being back in the old days, pissing about, before everything, and I'm allowed to enjoy it, I'm allowed to remember it without anything else creeping in.

And it probably would have done the trick and calmed

him down too, if Steph hadn't come over and tried giving me a hand.

As soon as she touches him he starts going berserk. An angry little skeleton on speed. And my hands do seem to pass right through him then 'cause he's away and on her in a flash, flailing his arms and screaming and trying to hit her. Oh fuck, I'm thinking. That woman's going to just love this – coming outside to find a lunatic hitting a girl. She'll have the army arriving soon. And the odd thing is that I don't stop him, not straight off. There's this moment where I wait. There's this moment where maybe I want him to hit her. And I want it to hurt.

When I grab him again I'm amazed at the energy stored up in that skinny frame. There's no real strength to it but it doesn't stop trying; there's a real dervish whirling and knocking about in it. He's clawing the air in front of Steph's face, which looks shocked, a kind of sad shocked, like some old dog you've walked past for years and patted on the head has suddenly turned and bitten you. I'm beginning to get worried that this dervish is going to keep at it right up until that woman appears again with the cavalry, and besides, it's a job and a half keeping hold of it and I'm not a hundred per cent certain I can. And I'm trying get a better hold, which is hard to do with a bunch of wriggling bones, when I end up tearing the rucksack off Neil's back. It comes off in my hand and the top rips open and these dried petals fly out into the air. That puts the brakes on it. For a second Neil goes skeleton-still, as still as a skeleton should be.

He watches the petals come fluttering down, veering gently this way and that like broken butterfly wings. He waits for them to fall. And when the last one touches the ground he crouches on his hands and knees and begins picking them up, carefully, one by one, as though he's collecting something dead valuable and delicate, a hummingbird's egg or something. He's making this whimpering noise and I find myself wanting to bend down and help him. And when I look up and see the woman staring at us from the door I don't care any more. I just want her to leave us alone. I want everyone to leave us alone.

Neil

They've broken you, Del.

I was trying to find them but Ricky wouldn't let me. I could see you waiting for me in my taid's yard. You were doing cartwheels and I could see the white triangle of your knickers, tern-white and wheeling in circles. And I was scared you wouldn't wait for me, but Ricky was holding me. And then Steph was trying to hold me. Steph was trying to make you go away again and I hated her for that. She let you go, Del. She left you. I was telling her not to leave you and then I was hitting her.

And then when I looked you were broken. You were in pieces. And I tried to put you back together but I couldn't. They've broken you, Del, and now you won't come back.

PART EIGHT

The Sea

Steph

Ricky said we had to go. The bell had just rung twelve which mean it was already five past.

We don't *have* to, I told him. And for a moment his face got hopeful and eager but I hadn't meant it like that. I meant we didn't have to do everything Del said. We could leave her.

Ricky didn't get it. His features were tensed in concentration. His lips were closed together, pushed out into a muzzling pout. I knew the look. Whenever Ricky had to think too much about something he made this extra effort to control his body and it showed on his face like the momentary grimace on a gymnast's before they leap. We'd be sitting on my bed and he'd be trying to edge closer – I knew he was, of course I did – but because he was having to plot each inch he'd start having little accidents. With his mind intent on reaching me, his limbs took their own twitchy course. My bedside lamp suffered, twice. A glass of water perished. A teddy bear lost an eye. It was as though he'd fallen out of one of the boats on my duvet and was thrashing his way towards an invisible shore. Not that I was invisible. And I could have made it easier, beamed a signal over the cotton waters, but maybe I didn't really want him to reach me. Maybe it was enough knowing that he was so desperate to.

We don't have to go, I said. And for a moment I watched him out of the corner of my eye like he was a creature from another element; a fish butting his head against the glass bottom of a boat, drawn helplessly to the oxygen glitter of the world that looked down on him from above.

'We better,' he said, getting up. 'They'll be waiting.' And suddenly the glass began to crack. Del was stamping on it with her big feet.

We set off through town. It was clear and sunny. It had been clear and sunny all week and the pensioners were beginning to clog the streets again. The light fell on their skin. It was pale and wrinkled and damp. I noticed their hands – the freckles, the liver spots, the way they trembled slightly when they reached out for things. I'd been noticing people's hands all day. They made me feel slightly sick but I couldn't stop looking at them. At breakfast I'd watched my dad scooping the top off a boiled egg and some of the soft, half-cooked white had fallen on to his knuckles and my stomach turned and I had to leave the room. 'What's wrong with her?' I heard him ask when I was gone. Even my dad's hands.

When we got to the edge of the green I didn't want to leave the pavement. Ricky thought I was playing around and tried to pull me on to the grass and I had to push him off. When he touched me it felt like I was spongy and porous and his fingers would go right through into my belly and guts. I hated it how the sun was shining. It was too bright. All around people were pretending to smile and their mouths looked contorted and misshapen in the light like the smiles on carnival masks or clowns, and sometimes I thought I saw their tongues flick out and taste the air. Ricky said it'd be quicker if we cut through the monkey woods and suddenly I didn't care. The town, the country, the village, they were all the same to me now. There wasn't any difference.

When we went through the fields I wasn't afraid of anything. The cows were cut out of cardboard and the walls were plasticine. When we reached the monkey woods I didn't flinch. The place Del and me had walked through before was gone. I listened to the chattering of the crows and looked up at the too bright sky through the waxy branches of the monkey trees and there was nothing to it, nothing but a few birds and pine needles. It was as if I was walking behind the tattered and pathetic scenery of an old ghost train. I couldn't believe that that had been us before. I wasn't in my own memory – another person was. Ricky kept stopping and waiting for me but he didn't have to. I didn't need to follow anyone any more.

When we went past his cottage I knew he was waiting for me in there. He'd told me I could come back whenever I wanted. He smiled when he said that. He smiled at me like I should be happy about it. The skin sagged off his face when he smiled like it was another face, melting away from his real one in the heat of that room. He said I could have whatever I wanted when I came back.

Ricky and me stopped for a minute on the road that went past Neil's grandparents' farm. There were two girls playing in the hay barn a hundred years ago. For a few seconds I began to think about them and then I started counting in my head instead and the numbers were endless. I could keep on counting for ever if I wanted to. Below us nothing was moving. It was a postcard. A landscape in a trance. The gulls were frozen in the air and the yachts on the straits were painted on the flat water. It was as though everything had stopped. Only the numbers were moving.

I kissed Ricky beside the saint's well. I wanted to know what it would feel like, I wanted the feel of it to wipe away the other feeling, but it didn't feel like anything. He was a fish wriggling under glass, with his slimy, suckery lips pressed against it. I began to count the coins at the bottom of the well.

'Why don't we wait here for a bit?' he asked.

'You're the one who said we *had* to go,' I told him.

'I didn't mean right away like,' he pleaded, but I didn't listen to him and carried on walking.

Del never waited for you. There'd be two knocks on your door and then she was off. Take it or leave it, thinking you'd always take it, thinking her infuriating confidence would trump every trick that got thrown down in front of her. Her sheer pig-headedness was amazing; believing it could bend the world into whatever shape it wanted, and then, if you were lucky, she'd let you shelter there. She'd offer you that, just the once, and then it was up to you – take it or leave it.

By the time Ricky and me got to the beach she was already in the boat. And the boat was already near the edge of the black rocks. She was trying to use the oars but they were long and heavy and she could barely pull them together on her own. The boat was moving slowly, veering in arcs to the left and then to the right, like she was trying to write a huge 'S' on the water. You could tell she couldn't keep her strokes together, that she was pulling too hard on the one oar and then over-compensating with the other; when my dad had taken me out in his boat I'd done the same and rowed in circles until he'd sat beside me and taken the other oar.

I looked across at the island. It looked further away today, satisfyingly far.

She wasn't going anywhere.

Neil was walking back and forth along the shore, following the movement of the boat the same way a dog does when its owner leaves it behind. Sometimes he'd go close to the water's edge, linger there for a second, and then pull back and carry on walking back and forth. Ricky called out to him but he didn't seem to hear us and we had to go over to him.

'She shouldn't go past the rocks,' he said as if he was talking to himself. 'She shouldn't. There's currents under the water.'

'She's not going to get far on her tod, is she?' Ricky said.

'She shouldn't. I told her.'

'She's going nowhere without someone else in that boat.'

Ricky waved and shouted out to Del but her eyes stayed fixed on the oars in front of her; fixed with a kind of childish and vexed determination, an infant's frustration with objects refusing to bend to its fumbling will. Try as she might, she couldn't get the square block into the triangular hole. And from where we stood she looked so small and puny in that boat – a baby crab trying to manoeuvre a shell that was far too big for it. Her lenses glinted under the light of the sun and you could see the pea-green wool of her jumper. Ricky shouted again.

'I told her to wait for you,' Neil said.

'You should have gone with her. She's going nowhere.'

'You said . . .'

As Neil and Ricky bickered I looked behind me and saw that a group of pensioners were standing beyond the rocks, facing the lighthouse. I hadn't noticed any coaches in the car park and I wondered if they'd been there all along. None of them were moving. They were just staring, with the blank, granitic eyes of statues. I could feel their sight on my skin and it made me shiver.

When I looked back Del had lost one of the oars. It must have come out of its lock and it was floating by the side of the boat. She dangled a hand over the side of the boat, trying to reach it, but she couldn't. Ricky shouted and this time she glanced up towards us, and you could just about make out her expression, that expression that said I don't need you, and then she leant over the side, reaching out further towards the oar. For a second her jumper lifted up her back, exposing a pale bulge of her flesh. And then she fell into the water.

When she began trying to swim I was surprised by how awkwardly she moved; she was so incongruously graceful on land that it was hard to recognize her as she started

thrashing about in the sea. It was an almost unfeasible trans-
formation. Maybe it was hard for the others to take in too.
Because for a while the three of us just stood there watching
her, as though she were a trapeze artist who'd missed her grip
and was suspended in that half second where their somer-
sault unfolds into their fall. She was aiming for the rocks but
however frenetically her arms moved she made no visible
progress towards them. And then she started moving slowly
backwards out of the bay and into the open sea.

Neil ran towards the rocks. When he got on to them he
kept slipping and stumbling and there was blood on his hands
where they'd scraped on the mussels and barnacles. He fell
into a rock pool and lay there in the water as if he couldn't
move. Ricky was close behind and when he stopped and tried
helping him out of it Neil was making a strange, hysterical
noise, a kind of high, wailing cry that was like nothing I'd
ever heard. Years later I'd hear a rabbit dying and it would
remind me of that noise.

Ricky and me got to the edge of the rocks first and by now
Del was about ten or fifteen feet away. The movement of her
arms had slowed down, as if she was resigned to the fact that
nothing she did with them any more was going to propel her
forwards. They flopped in front of her in desultory, paddling
motions that barely upset the surface of the water. And for a
moment it seemed like nothing was moving again. We were
in the serene, static confines of a picture. A sun-washed holiday snap. A little girl floating in the sea, her hand lifted up
in greeting towards her two friends, while a third plays
behind them in a rock pool. The blue sky above them inked
here and there with the elongated 'M's of gull's wings and
criss-crossed by the thin white lines of aeroplane trails.
Except that if the you looked closely the water was rippling,
and through its surface you could see the weeds being pulled
out horizontally from the side of the rocks and swayed

violently back and forth. The water was moving. It seemed to be moving in different directions all at once.

The boat was drifting towards the end of the rocks and the lighthouse, but the oar had come to rest against a semi-submerged rock just below us. Ricky scrabbled down and tried to reach it. The swell came up over his knees and for a second I thought he'd jump backwards to safety, like in the game on the pier. But he didn't. With one hand grasping a clump of seaweed, he swung himself out into the water and grabbed the oar with the other.

By this time Del had been dragged further along and Ricky pulled himself back up beside me, clutching the oar, and followed her. The water seemed to have turned and had brought her in a few feet closer to the rocks. As Ricky lay down on his stomach and pushed the oar out towards her I looked at her face. It was so close now I could see the uneven strands of her hair plastered on her forehead and the little mole at the corner of her lips, which were opening and closing although she didn't have the breath to speak. I could hear Neil whimpering behind us and the sound seemed to come from her mouth not his. Her glasses had come off and her eyes looked shrunken and puffy like a pig's. Her arms had almost stopped moving altogether. Only her hands were really moving. Opening and closing, clutching at the water, reaching out for us. Ricky had pushed the oar out as far as he could. Half his body was in the water and he was holding the end of it with his fingertips. The other end was only inches from Del's grasp.

'Leave it,' I said.

And momentarily Ricky turned his head around to face me.

'Leave it,' I said. And for a second he paused, staring up at me. And in that second, whether it was from the pull of the water or a relaxation in his grip, the oar slipped out of his fingers. Then Del and the oar were both being pulled out together. She was still reaching for it with her hands.

The water took her past the far edge of the rocks, moving quickly now, and Neil and Ricky ran there and stood watching as it took her into the straits and past the lighthouse. Neil ran right to the edge. He ripped his jacket and shoes off and stood on the edge as if about to dive. He swayed there for a while, his pale, bare feet twitching on the rock, and then he turned back and looked up to where the group of pensioners stood and opened his mouth in one long and silent scream.

I watched her head bob up and down in the water as I counted the lighthouse chimes. One, two. And by three her head was gone. But I could still see her hands opening and closing. And I would have held them, Del. I wanted to. I'd always wanted to. And if you'd let me I would have. I wanted you to hold me and I was furious that you didn't. I was furious that you never did anything I wanted you to do. And then you left me behind. I thought about you when he touched me, Del. I want you to know that. Even though that changes nothing. Even though in the end I could never really leave you behind.

Ricky

Of course here's me in a rush and she's off with the fairies again. Except I don't reckon fairies are going to have a problem with walking on a bit of grass. Steph's a Rubik's cube, she really is. Turn her one way and the colours all fit, turn her the other and they're all mixed up. And you don't quite know how the hell you did either and so you don't know what it's going to end up looking like next time you give it a go. Sometimes you just want to peel off the stickers and put them back where you want them to be. And sometimes you just want to chuck it in the bin.

We're on the pavement by the green and she's stopped. I'm standing there in front of her doing my citrus impression, Ricky the lemon, and she's oohing and aahing about walking on the grass. They're a nice pair of shoes, I'll grant her that, but if she's so worried about getting them muddy, then why's she wearing them? We're off on a boat trip, for fuck's sake. Does she think they're going to stay dry and clean? First she wants to go, then she doesn't, then she does, then she doesn't. This is doing my head in. I'd like to just grab her and drag her – or even better, just bugger off on my own. Those church bells have gone and they're late and we're late.

But can I? Can I have one thought that doesn't have her creeping into it? No. I'll end up taking two steps and both those steps are going to be *away* from Steph. Not *to* anywhere. Honestly, my brain's like one of them garden mazes these days, an absolutely frigging predictable one. Decide to go one way – and there's Steph. Decide to go the other way – and there's Steph. And there's no thread leading me out of it either, only a big fucking rope that I'm all tied up in. I reach out and try pulling her on to the grass and she palms me off sharpish.

We'll take a short cut, I decide. I tell her that, but of course I'm asking her. And I'm expecting her to say no – she won't even come on to the green – but instead she starts following me towards the monkey woods as happy as you like. She's everywhere in the maze and I'm always lost in it.

She starts out behind me and she ends up in front of me. She practically runs through the woods. When we pass by the mansion there's a flock of crows standing around on the roof and in the windows, yattering at each other, nodding their heads up and down like they're straining to push the loudest croak possible out of their beaks. One of them starts it and then the rest all get in on the act. You call that a croak, here's a croak, here's a caw that'll have your feathers standing up on end. And when we go past they take off and wing it over the woods, croaking and cawing, and even when they're too far away for me to be actually hearing them any more, I can. And I can hear Del too. You're not going to. You're not going to. You're not going to. But how do you know that? And why bother saying it? And how many conversations do we end up having with people afterwards, when they're not there; with them croaking and cawing in our head like it's a big empty mansion and us croaking and cawing back when there's nobody to hear it, nobody to listen. When there's nobody there.

Steph's practically sprinting when we go past the gatehouse. It's a job keeping up. Not so precious about her shoes now, I guess. One minute she won't shift off the pavement, the next she's scarpering along through the woods like a gazelle. What I'd give for an easy day out, I'm thinking, a Disney day out: holding hands; a few butterflies and blue-birds floating about (whatever bluebirds are – but they sound nice); Steph dolled up like Little Red Riding Hood or some-thing, carrying a picnic basket; a couple of friendly deer coming out to bat their eyelashes at us; and sod it, why not throw Llew in as well – maybe with a pair of cute cubs to keep him company, and a huge jar of honey? But no. Here's me instead, with a flock of crows above me, having an argu-ment with someone in my head, chasing after a girl who suddenly can't stay within ten paces of me, off on some stupid fucking trip to an island in a nicked boat. I mean, what was Del on about pretending she'd found it? I'd stood right beside the fucker in the Robinsons' garden. Why do that? What's she trying to prove? And why do I have to ask all these things when I've never had to before, not with her? I mean, fuck, I don't know where the hell I am with everything else, so why does it have to be the same with her, when I always used to know where I was with her?

When I go past the Candyman's he's there in the window. He's trying to be a sly one, peeping through the curtains, but I spot him. It's like he's waiting for us, like he's expecting us to come knocking. And if we did I'd quite like to ask him when all of this finished: these goose chases that don't get you anywhere but you can't stop making. And if I did he'd prob-ably look at me with his damp eyes and lift his livery hand to his chin and say some crap like, 'Ah, the tribulations of young love,' when what I meant was all of it, not just that. It's all right for him, living in there with his stuffed spaniel. This shit's well behind him.

When we get to Seiriol's Well Steph kisses me. She comes up and cups her hand around the back of my head and starts kissing me. Her eyes are shut and her lips are moving slowly and carefully, as though she's looking with them instead. And for a second or two I'm thinking this is so simple and it's all I wanted and if I concentrate then I can't think about anything else. This is the lost I wanted. I'm keeping my eyes open to make sure it's happening and I can see the coins glittering in the well and it's like I've got the jackpot; all the lemons have spun into place and the tray's filling up. And it's worth the hundreds of pounds I've put into the slot – the bonus lights I couldn't work out, the higher or lower gambles I got wrong, the nudges that got me nowhere. It was worth it. For this glitter of coins which is the colour of her hair as it falls over my face and the feel of lips that make you feel nothing else. And I should close my eyes too. I really should. Because if I do then I won't be able to see the way her face looks. It's scrunched and rigid as if she's checking, practising, experimenting, giving it a spin to see what shows up, as if I'm a frigging pillow in her bedroom and not a part of this kiss at all. And then I'm not.

She says, 'Let's get going.' And I say . . . and then I give up.

Del's made a start without us. She's out there in the boat with her specs glinting in the sun like big round blinking eyes. The owl's set off without the pussycat. He's still on the beach, wandering back and forth and fucking useless.

He's gibbering about currents and shit and I tell him why didn't you go with her, she's going nowhere on her own. And she's not. She twitching about in the bay like a fly in a puddle with a broken wing. For Christ's sake, Neil, I say. Only it's pointless 'cause he's gibbering more nonsense and 'cause what I'm really saying is why didn't I go with her?

Del, I shout. I want her just to turn around and come back. I'll go with her, it's not a problem. But I can't tell if she hears me and whether she's trying to turn around or head further out. She's moving sideways in little half-circles, this way and that.

Del, I shout. And then for the first time I realize that I
don't think she knows what she's doing or where she's going.
She's flailing and floundering. She really is at sea. And there's
this nervy, sick feeling beginning to churn and spin about in
my belly, as if I've swallowed a washing machine, and it's
making my legs weak and trembly. On the outside everything's looking as still and calm as you like – the sun's up there
smiling, the sky's cloudless and solid blue, the island and the
mainland are fast asleep, the old folks standing further along
the shore are comatose, the birds are making the air seem like
it's amber, the water's flat, the whole world's flat – but inside
it's swaying and tilting and circling and it feels like I'm about
to fall off it. Del, I shout. But she's already in the water.

It's four, maybe five, inches away. If my arm was longer
it'd reach her easy. And I'm trying, I'm honestly fucking
trying. My arm's almost out of its socket I'm trying so hard.
To begin with, all I'm thinking is four or five inches. My face
is right beside the water, my nose is touching it, and what was
in my stomach is under its surface: the seaweed's careering
around, the mussel beds and barnacles seem to be quaking,
and there's these bits and flecks of I don't know what tumbling and somersaulting into where it gets too deep and dark
and far away to see. Four or five inches I think, 'cause if I
think any further then I'll be following them.

I try not to look at Del. Her specs have gone and her eyes
seem helpless, the way people's eyes do when they first take
their specs off. Those blinking, face-scrunching seconds when
they're like little creatures dragged out of their glass caves
into the daylight. I try not to look 'cause if I do then I don't
reckon I'll be able to hold on to the oar and the rock. Her
arms are treading the water, slowly and sort of hopelessly, as
though they don't quite believe in what they're doing any
more, as though they're amazed that this stuff they're moving
through can actually hold them back, that it's real and it's

called their bluff. It's there in her face too: the amazement, the shock. And when I see it it's like I'm slipping off too, like I've suddenly realized that I'm only kidding myself I can do this, like I'm some shit magician who's stopped believing in his tricks at the last moment and ended up cutting the girl in the box in half. And somewhere in my head Del's telling me that as well. The top bit of the torso, shouting you're not going to, you're not going to. And maybe I'm not, though I can't work out whether she's telling me this or asking me this. But I'm fucking furious with her for saying it.

'Leave her,' Steph says.

And I don't know if I did or I didn't.

'Leave her,' she says.

And the next second the oar's gone out of my fingers.

There's nothing I can do then, except watch her go. Her head bobs up and down and the gulls go screeching crazily above her, holding those high, long, outraged notes in their beaks for a moment before they putter out into the low, broken, fading ones. The aftermath ones. The ones that make you feel like everything that was in front of you is suddenly behind you. I can hear the lighthouse chimes too. One, two, three of them. But they don't sound separate. They sound like one noise, a warning siren wailing in my ear. And what do you do in those last few minutes before it all ends? I'll tell you.

You do fuck all. That's what you do. You stand on a rock under a sun and a sky and watch it all disappear.

Neil

We walk together to the beach, with the leaves beginning to open along the hedgerows and the daffodils' petals beginning to curl and rot above their stems. Two early swallows dart fast through the sycamore branches and then up into the blue of the sky. They move so fast they make me dizzy. I wish I was old like my taid and then my eyes would slow them down. Because he says your eyes slow down with your body, that they stretch out time when you don't have much of it left.

It's almost one o'clock and I don't want it to be. I don't want us to arrive on the beach and I don't want us to get to the boat. But Del walks so quickly and when I try to stop or dawdle she doesn't wait for me.

When we get to the beach the others aren't there. Only the old people are there. They're walking slowly towards the shore opposite the lighthouse, so slowly that it's like they'll never reach it. Their feet move tremblingly through every step and I wonder if they see things like my taid says he sees them, and that for them the oystercatchers and gulls are creeping over the sea and the chimes of the lighthouse are hours and hours away, when I know that for me they are only minutes away because it's almost one o'clock and they will chime every half hour. I think I can smell them. Mixed in with the scent of the salt and the stones there is another one, of damp cloth and coal smoke and meat left too long on the table. And when I stare closely I can see the wetness gathering in the corners of their eyes, as if they are turning into water.

The first chime comes. Del and me are standing beside the branches and the boat is under them. The others aren't here. When the third chime comes it will be one o'clock. Ricky's at Steph's. Ricky's always at Steph's and he thinks we don't know that. Steph's jealous because she thinks Ricky likes Del more than her. She made Ricky laugh at Del and I hated her for that.

The third chime comes and Del begins lifting the branches off the boat. I wish that somebody else had found it and taken it away. The sea feels cold. Even from up here on the top of the beach you can feel that it is cold. It leaves its coldness on the stones like it leaves it on skin. This sun doesn't warm them. Del asks me to give her a hand pulling the boat and I say we should wait for the others. Come on, Neil, she says. And I say we should wait for Ricky and she says it doesn't matter, that we don't need their help with the boat. They'll be coming anyway. And I say . . . Suit yourself, she says, and starts trying to pull it by herself. But the wheels of the trailer are stuck and it won't move. Del keeps pulling. Her jumper comes up over her jeans and the skin of her back is the colour and smoothness of the stones and I worry that the sea is cooling it and I want to tug the jumper back down to protect it. If I don't help her, I think. If I don't. But she won't give up and her face is going red and her breath is getting heavy and I can't stop myself.

I let go at the water's edge and retreat back up the stones. Del pulls the trailer into the sea, going in up to her knees. When she comes out her jeans are stuck to her legs and the muscles of her calves look too small and slender to carry her.

She sits down on the beach and I sit beside her. Her hair hangs crookedly over her ear and the sun has brought out freckles on her cheek. The wool of her jumper smells warm and I want to press my face against it and close my eyes. I want us to sit here all day, to do nothing but sit here until the tide has taken the sea far away and left us alone. But she won't sit still. Beneath her jumper her body is fidgeting and her hands keep moving – up to her face, on to her neck, across her thighs – and her lips are drawn together impatiently and her tongue keeps flicking out over the top one and she bites the bottom one with her teeth. She's staring at the island and through her lenses her eyes look bigger than they are, like the island is making them bigger. She won't sit still.

'Let's go,' she says. 'They're late.'

But we should wait for them, I tell her.

'They're not coming,' she says. 'We don't need them anyway.'

But they will come, I tell her. And I'm thinking if they don't then we can just sit here. If I can pretend they will and then they don't we can . . .

Del's starts untying the bow of the boat from the trailer. She undoes the knots quickly. They melt in her fingers. Nothing ever stops her. The boat's in the water now and she's holding it with the rope. The old people should stop us but they just stand there, as still as the mainland and the mountains across the straits which seem to be sleeping under a green quilt. Under the bridge the sailors never sleep, they swirl in circles in the underwater caves and never close their eyes and never stop. My taid told me.

'Come on then,' Del says. 'Get in.'

I don't say anything.

'We don't have to wait for them. Look, Neil,' she says, and her voice is soft and steady like it will pick me up and put me safely in the boat and take me anywhere. 'Look, Neil, it's not far, is it? It's nothing.'

But I can see the water holding on to her ankles and creeping towards her knees.

'Please, Neil. I can't row it properly on my own.'

But I can already feel it in my lungs and it's acid and it's burning into my stomach.

There's currents, I want to say. They're under the surface and they go sideways and down. But I know she won't be frightened of them. They'll be like ghosts to her and she won't believe in them.

'Please, Neil.'

I can't, I say. I can't. And I don't know if the words have come out of my mouth. My lungs are full and there's no breath in them.

'That's OK,' she says. 'You don't have to.'

Then she's in the boat and it's moving out towards the rocks. The gulls are watching now. They look down from above and their eyes are yellow and the bottom of their beaks are specked with blood. The others are here and I tell them there's currents. I say I tried to make her wait but she wouldn't. I say . . . and then she's in the water. And I don't know where I am. For a while I'm in the water too, and it's burning my skin and making it bleed and the weeds won't let me go. And when I escape from it Steph's letting Del go. She's making Ricky leave her in the sea.

And the sea takes her. It takes her quickly, past the edge of the rocks and into the straits between Seiriol's Island and the shore. I run after her. To the edge of the rocks. Why won't she wait for me? I don't want her to go and she knows I can't follow her in there. Into the sea. I try to but I can't. I try to. And then she's gone and I want her to come back. Her head comes back for a second. It's there and then it's not there. And I turn to shout at the old people but they don't hear me. And they don't see her. And then she's gone.

I look everywhere and she's gone. And the green of the fields behind me, the green of the island in front of me, the green of the mainland and the mountains across the straits, the green of the leaves beginning to open on the trees – it's the green of mould growing on a suddenly dead and burnt and wet and acid-blackened world.

PART NINE

Departures

Steph

My face stings where Neil hit me. Above my left cheekbone, on the side of my jaw, on my bottom lip. I think this is what he wanted to do, the whole way here. Poor Neil. Neil, who had to wait all this time to do it, when he could have done it that day. But he didn't. Instead he ran along the coast, following the straits as if he were still following her, even though we didn't know where she was going then. He ran as far as the town and by that time the fishing boat must have found her. And I don't know how he knew to wait there, on the beach below the pier, for the hour or so it took them to bring her back on to the shore; how he knew that that was where they'd land her.

Ricky and me watched him run but we didn't go after him, not straight away. Ricky sat down on the rocks and I stood facing Seiriol's Island. After a while Ricky got up and started walking towards town. He didn't say anything to me. I let him get ahead of me, almost out of sight, before I moved.

We were both there when they brought her in. We didn't know where they'd bring her in either, but because Neil was waiting beneath the pier we waited as well. Not together. Close by but not together. At first we were the only ones there – before the ambulance and the cars and the people came – waiting like gulls wait above the water, knowing where the shoals of fish will be before the fishermen know. I watched the boat come in and I watched the man jump on to its deck and hold Del's wrist in his hand, like the Candyman had held my wrist.

It stings, and I wonder if this is the reason he found me and wrote to me; clenching his pen in his thin, bony fist while he imagined it thudding against my skin. It arrived on a Saturday afternoon, the letter. It said when and where, that's all, and could I tell Ricky (how was I supposed to find him? How had he found me?). But I think he knew I'd come. For weeks afterwards I began to see things I'd not noticed before – withered bunches of flowers on roadsides, photographs curled around the iron railings of fences, children's toys hidden carefully in parks – and looking at them I realized what I already knew: that it's always the last place that we remember, that we go to, always the last place and not necessarily the one allotted to us for remembering. Maybe time counts for more than we think with the dead. Maybe it becomes distance, so that in following them back to their final minutes and seconds we get closer to them somehow. Maybe the last place is the nearest place.

When they lifted her into the ambulance she was already gone. The thing they carried off the boat was no more to me than one of the gutted fish on its decks. I turned away and walked on my own into town, past the castle walls, along the main street and my father's shop, up Rosemary Lane where the old women waited by the post office, and on to Stanley Road, between the rows of little elves' cottages which were painted happy colours and pretended to be houses. And I kept thinking of the invisible people in the woods and fields and hills beyond, those spectres who I'd sometimes sensed were watching me here and who perhaps now were; as if I had finally become one of their invisible children too, left to stalk furtively the streets that had been taken away from them, that they had never been allowed to belong to. Nobody on these streets seemed to see me.

When I went into my house my mother was sitting in the living room, dressed up like she was about to go out. Her make-up was done and she was wearing her fur coat. But she wasn't going out. She did this some days. She'd huff and puff around the house, picking clothes out of cupboards and then putting them back, emerging from the bathroom in a cloud of steam and perfume, until at last she was perfect and ready. And then she'd sit down in the living room, as though she were waiting for someone to arrive and pick her up. She'd sit there for the whole day until eventually, when I came home from school or my father got back from the shop, she'd stomp back up the stairs into her bedroom like she'd been stood up. Sometimes she'd do this day after day for weeks and never leave the house, not once.

'Where have you been?' she asked. It's what she always asked.

'Nowhere.'

'So where's nowhere today then?'

'Nowhere.'

There were two ways this could go. If I was unlucky she could wheedle at me for the next few minutes like it was terribly important that she knew, like she was a doctor trying to root out the source of an infection. If I was lucky she'd stomp up the stairs straight away.

Today I was lucky.

Up in my own room I couldn't get the smells off me. I tried. I took the perfume I'd stolen from my mother and poured it over my clothes but it didn't make any difference. They were still on me. There was Del's smell, a faint mix of chip oil and hay dust and the heavy wool of her jumpers, and then there was his smell, a lingering reek of mould spores and dampness and stagnant brine. I opened the window hoping the fresh April air would wash them off, but it didn't and I started counting again in my head to make them go away. And for days afterwards I did nothing but count and because I couldn't sleep I must have reached millions and millions. And maybe I'd already started counting the days before I could leave, before I could run away. I don't know. But it did seem, as I stared out my window, that with each number I reached the town outside became less and less real, that its solidity drained out of it until it was nothing more than a rickety shanty of painted balsa wood, and that if I was to blow on it then it would all fall down. And perhaps it did too. Perhaps that would explain how easily I let it go.

Even during those first, hard years, when I was on my own and didn't know where to go, I discovered others like me – if you look closely then you find them everywhere and I'd learnt to look closely by then, because you do when you're on your own – but most of them carried with them some recollection of what they'd left behind; a place remembered, if only in hate and fear and bitterness and anger. But I carried nothing with me. I razed my mind into a flat, horizonless plain, and was surprised how quickly and effortlessly the town and everything in it toppled out of view. What remained was no more than a few wisps of smoke rising out of the rubble. Nothing. Or almost nothing.

A saint's well, a beach of white stones, a lighthouse, an island off the coast of an island – we're here and they're as real to me as the stinging on my face. They never stopped being real. Year after year after year they never stopped. I walked to them every day and however far away they got in time that didn't stop me reaching them. The last place is the nearest place.

He knew I'd come. And I think she did too.

Ricky

Whatever got into Neil it's got out of him now. He traipses past the well and the dovecote, holding on to his bag hellish tightly like it's a sack full of monkeys as mad as him. He's left Steph's face in a bit of a state; there's red on her cheek and her lip's swelling but she's not making any fuss about it. In fact she's right there beside him. Only an arm's length away.

I have to admit I've got a guilty secret about that well. When I was a kid I nicked a load of coins out of it. You couldn't blame me, they were just lying there and I needed a few pennies to buy a pack of pickled onion Monster Munch. At the time I didn't feel guilty at all. I mean, Seiriol didn't need them, did he, sitting up there in heaven with Cybi? And who else was going to use them? It dropped out of my head about as fast as the coins went over the counter in Spar. But then a few weeks later I started thinking of it and I couldn't stop myself. I thought how they were meant to be lucky, those coins, and people made wishes with them, and so maybe I hadn't just nicked some stray coppers, I'd nicked a whole pocketful of other people's luck. I tried to get around it. I mean, what exactly were the rules with lucky coins? Did you get your luck the moment the coin hit the water? Or did they have to sit on the bottom for a while before the well shelled it out, like a bank paying interest or something? I didn't know. But I couldn't get around it and it started throbbing in my head, the idea of me having nicked this luck. Then the guilt came. I kept imagining that there was some bloke somewhere who was walking out in front of a car or slipping off a ladder at that very second, and that if he'd got his couple of pence worth then he'd of waited that moment longer on the kerb or put his foot a few inches to the left or right. And in a way that was my fault. I'd taken it. And the other thing was that I hadn't noticed myself getting that much luckier into the bargain. So what if it worked itself out and the well took my luck instead, in compensation? How much would I have to pay back? Would I be doling it out for ever? And all for a pack of fucking Monster Munch! I couldn't believe it – that I'd done this one little thing without even thinking about it and now it was there in the back of my brain all the time and it wouldn't go away. It was like I'd swallowed one of them puffer fish reckoning it was just a tiny minnow and then it'd swelled up into a huge, big, round fucker in my guts and I was never going to get it out.

If it'd make a jot of difference I'd go over to that well right now and chuck a hundred quid in it. But I don't think it works that way.

Neil and Steph carry on until they reach the beach. Look at them, walking side by side. You'd reckon they were a couple off on a seaside stroll, taking in the fresh air and the views. And if they were, then the island's put on a hell of show for them today. The straits are laid out flat under that light that I've never seen anywhere else, dead still, dead calm, but not quite dead, not really – a kind of hovering, hushed, slow light that makes you feel as if you're waiting for something even though you don't know what it is. And the mountains and the Orme and Seiriol's Island, well, they're all waiting with you too; and you're feeling like this world is only a picture and you can see its edges and it's about to be lifted aside. And the one behind it is even more beautiful. I've never seen anything like it, honestly. And wherever I am it's there. But how do you tell people that? How do you explain it?

And how do you explain how scared you get that you've lost it? That there's days when your stomach begins hurting for no reason and there's this place that you love but you're suddenly afraid to go there. It's sick and aching and you're thinking how maybe five inches became a billion fucking miles and you won't be able to get back. And something takes all the roads and borders and electricity in your head and squeezes them into a molten fist that bruises and burns you. I don't know if I did or I didn't, Del. If I let go of it on purpose or not. I don't know if I might have reached you. But I didn't mean to let you go. I didn't. And this place is all I've got left of you, Del, this one place, and if I can't love it then you're gone for ever.

Steph

Neil walks with me down towards the edge of the water. It laps the stones, quietly and gently, and I stop just before reaching it. He looks sideways at me for an instant, but he knows this is as far as I'll go with him. He pauses, clenches his bag, stares at his feet, and then he walks into it, moving so slowly that it takes an age for it to climb over his shoes and cover his ankles. He inches forward, up to his knees, and then stops to lean against the black rock by his side, trembling and swaying like the seaweed beneath him. He closes his eyes and waits, and everything seems to wait with him. The gulls are quiet above us and the boats have stalled on the horizon. Even the lighthouse chimes, which I keep expecting, don't arrive. I don't know how long we wait. But eventually he lets go of the rock and wades further into the water, past his waist and almost up to his chest, holding his bag out in front of him. Then he stops again and opens the bag and throws the rose petals into the sea. They lie still on its surface for a moment before the current slowly takes them, spreading them out into a wide circle and then carrying them away, past the rocks and out of the bay, past the lighthouse and into the straits, until we can't see them any more. Then the chimes arrive. One by one by one.

Ricky

I think it's OK. As Neil goes into the sea I hold on to Llew's claw and I think it's OK. It's like he's holding my hand and he leads me along the beach, ambling through the seaweed and the sunshine, a skip in his step and a smile on his snout. It is beautiful, he says. It always was and it's yours, Ricky. It's yours. And as long as we're here then we're all still together. Welcome back, he says. Croeso yn ôl.

Neil

We went down towards the sea, the three of us, away from
the thin green covering of the land and over the white stones
of the beach. The sun cast a soft film of light over the air and
held it breathless and still, so that the birds seemed to strug-
gle to move through it, flapping their wings slowly like manta
rays. And I realized then that I was tired. Like I had been
tired that day with the bike, trying to ride it through the mud,
as though this ground too were becoming viscous and liquid,
a pearly froth that pulled on my ankles and drained the
muscles of my legs. I could feel Steph close beside me and I
was tired of hating her, exhausted by it, and I couldn't stop
myself feeling the warmth of her shoulder where it nearly
touched mine. For so long I'd imagined that moment the
other way around, with Del on the shore and Steph in the
sea, with Del leaving her, but I couldn't any more. Steph's
flesh had been firm against my fists and it was only Steph
who was here now, with me, in this time.

Steph and Ricky, who stopped behind me as I walked to
the water's edge, without pausing or halting, tired and
exhausted of being afraid, entering it effortlessly with limbs
that no longer had the strength for fear and hating. As it rose
over my feet and legs I felt a strange relief, the resignation
that a runner must feel when he realizes that he can't run any
further. They say we began as dust, but the earth began as

water and it will end as water and there will be nowhere to hide from it then.

It was only my tiredness that made me stop, for a minute or two, to lean against a rock and rest my legs and eyes. And with my eyes closed and my hand against the rock it was like being in a cave and I remembered when they took us to the mines at Blaenau Ffestiniog. The school bus drove us over the bridge. We went through Bethesda and into the Ogwen Valley and I stared out the window thinking how this must be the oldest place in the world. The mountains were like Jack Cucu's teeth, carious and geriatric; abraded, grey-brown stumps. They were huddled under an umbrella of mist, looking mutely back at me with creased and rubbled faces, the scree sprouting like cancer spots on their skin. Mr Jones pointed them out and named them for us. But I was glad when we'd passed them by and dropped down into the woods near Betws-y-Coed. Seeing them had only made me think of how long everything lasted, of how long it clung on. It almost made me shudder to know these mountains would be waiting for us when we drove back. In a million years they would still be there.

If the Ogwen Valley was the oldest place in the world then Blaenau was the saddest. It was a ruin of slate. The mountains here were all turned inside out and rows of stone houses crouched beneath their eviscerated bellies, in the shadow of their slagged guts. The slates on the roofs looked like blue-black drops of the mountain's blood.

In the town I saw two men walking up the street, their backs stooped and their eyes pointed mournfully ahead, as though they were bearing the whole place in a box upon their shoulders. A dog with no tail was licking water out of a puddle.

Mr Jones and Miss Roberts herded us into the yellow box cars and we trundled down into the entrance shaft. The glow of bulbs replaced the grey daylight and flickered over wooden slats and beams and veins and tendons of wire. And then there was only wet and naked rock. The tunnel walls were dripping. The mountain was still bleeding. Somewhere above us a disembodied voice told us that this was how the miners went to work and how they got the slate to the surface. It was a boy's voice. Then it went quiet and the only sound was the wheels turning on their axles and running along the steel of the tracks.

Ricky and Del were sitting in front of me. Their faces were lit up intermittently, flitting in and out of view. For a second I shut my eyes and their faces lingered against the blackness behind my lids, forming hard, mineral shapes – diamonds, crystals, cones – before merging into a single white triangle, oscillating across the darkness. Back and forth it went. And then up and down too. A will-o'-the-wisp that I tried to follow but which eventually disappeared into the liquid murk behind my sockets. It had seemed familiar.

Two weeks before I'd been standing at the bottom of the schoolyard beside the outside toilets, where I often waited at break-times, half because I could slip inside them to hide and half because I was willing myself to want to go, to go then and not later when I'd have to ask. But it hardly ever worked. The damp, mossy green of the tiles seemed to freeze something inside of me and nothing would come out, even though later I knew it would thaw and burn and ache. I was watching some of the older boys playing football (careful to keep my eyes slightly averted, to avoid paying the price of a caught gaze – What are you looking at? Go on, say it . . . say it!) when that same triangle had appeared against the yard's far wall. It was Del.

She was doing cartwheels. She was doing one after another, in rapid succession, and each time she spun over on to her hands the black nylon of her skirt would crumple up her thighs and the white triangle of her knickers would shine against the grey limestone of the wall. It wheeled and scintillated and seemed momentarily beyond the capacity of the yard to contain it, spinning free of the pitted concrete and the walls and the pebble-dashed buildings, free of the island's wet fields and drizzled horizons, free of everything: a soft white spirit dancing unencumbered through the air. And as I watched it I felt free of them too. It arced closer towards me and I knew I shouldn't stare but I couldn't help myself. It was as though there was a kind of safety in watching it, that it existed in a world of unextinguishable light – beyond eclipse, beyond submergence, beyond the dark – and that if you kept following it you could be there with it. And then it had become Del, peering at me through the lenses of her glasses.

'What are you looking at?'

I'd crashed back down on to the yard. I tried to say sorry.

'You all right?'

I was trying to say sorry. I could hear the bell ringing to call us back to class.

'Come on then, come with me.'

She took my hand and led me towards the school buildings. As we approached the entrance my tongue felt suddenly buoyant in my mouth.

'Thank you,' I said.

'It's all right.'

When I opened my eyes we'd come to a stop in a huge cave. It was lit from below, with big square lights, which reached upwards like search beams in a war film, illuminating an arching stone sky. The voice had returned and the boy was talking about his first day in the mine; how the darkness, filled with smoke from candles and sulphur from spent dynamite, had made him imagine that he'd entered the hell his minister had described for him in chapel. But as he went on it turned into another hell: a hell of dangerous, subterranean lives. Long days, hours of hard labour, accidents. Widows. Children with no fathers. Fathers with no fingers. Whenever you see a piece of slate, he told us, think of me.

The air smelt wet and ferric. Mr Jones was arranging us into an orderly line. Two by two we were supposed to go, animals into an underground ark. Stay away from the fences, he said, frowning as the boy's voice continued with its litany of calamities. *Perygl* said the signs on the fences. I was trying to move ahead in the line so I could walk beside Del. I could see her in front of me, swinging her arms as she went, crunching her shoes into the gravel path, the earth secure and sturdy beneath her feet. I waited for Mr Jones to stop fussing and then attempted to creep along the side of the line towards her. But beneath my feet the ground was more treacherous. Chunks of slate jutted out and tried to trip me. Some of the other children's feet did too. I carried on though, making good progress. I'd got past three pairs of children and could have almost touched the jagged, uneven bangs of Del's hair when I slipped on a piece of slate and veered a few yards to my left. I brushed against one of the chain fences and its sign began to sway. I hadn't known what the *perygl* was until I looked over.

Below me a shaft plummeted abruptly down, fifty or sixty feet, into a pool of water. Its surface was obsidian. Its sides were sheer as glass. Nothing that fell into it would ever get back out. I don't know how long I stood there. I couldn't hear the boy's voice any more, and although in the corner of my vision Mr Jones was moving towards me with his mouth open, shouting, I couldn't hear that either. I couldn't hear anything, only the dripping of water getting louder and louder until it roared like a cataract in my ears. And then abruptly even that was gone. I stared down into the pool and what I saw there was an absolute silence, inviolate and everlasting, out of which no sound could ever escape. I felt the weight of the old, crippled hills pressing down upon me, the hills that would stagger on for a million years, and a million years after that, but in the end would topple into this pool, like everything else would: every word, every voice, every stone, everything I'd ever seen or heard, everything I'd ever loved.

This time when I opened my eyes the bay was in front of me. The lighthouse stood off the shore and Seiriol's Island waited in the distance. I walked out further until the water pressed against my ribs. Then I stopped again and I threw the rose petals into the water and watched as the sea took them away. They eddied and circled over the surface before disappearing into the straits. And then the lighthouse bell let out a chime and a flock of dunlins and turnstones flickered into the air in front of me, arcing up towards the sky. For a second I'd wanted to follow the petals, to let myself slip from the stones beneath my feet and go with them to wherever they were going. But I didn't. I turned around and came back.

property of
The Blue Mountains
Public Library
L.E. Shore Memorial Library
Thornbury, Ontario N0H 2P0

PICADOR

....& more

**Talk about books with us,
our authors, other readers,
bloggers, booksellers
and others at
www.picador.com**

You can also:

- find out what's new at Picador

- read extracts from recently
  published books

- listen to interviews with
  our authors

- get exclusive special offers
  and enter competitions